THE RELUCTANT HEIR

Peter and Jean are an ordinary young couple planning to marry as soon as they can. But then comes the summons to Arachnock Castle on a remote Hebridean island, and they soon find that Peter's formidable grandfather has other plans. Two lives are to be turned upside down in the space of a few weeks, but will Peter and Jean find the happiness they seek?

Books by Grace Richmond
in the Linford Romance Library:

GRACE RICHMOND

THE RELUCTANT HEIR

Complete and Unabridged

LINFORD

Leicester

First Linford Edition
published August 1990

British Library CIP Data

Richmond, Grace, *1907*–
The reluctant heir.—Large print ed.—
Linford romance library
Rn: John Marsh I. Title
823′.912[F]

ISBN 0-7089-6948-8

Published by
F. A. Thorpe (Publishing) Ltd.
Anstey, Leicestershire
Set by Rowland Phototypesetting Ltd.
Bury St. Edmunds, Suffolk
Printed and bound in Great Britain by
T. J. Press (Padstow) Ltd., Padstow, Cornwall

1

JEAN CLAYTON knew there was something wrong as soon as Peter joined her at the table in the little café that Saturday morning.

His grey eyes were worried. He gave her an uneasy smile as he slipped into a seat by her side.

They had met to have a cup of coffee before going to look at some furniture at a local store. They were getting married in a month's time and most Saturday mornings were given up to buying things for their new home.

But it was not about tables and chairs that Peter spoke after the waitress had brought his cup of coffee. He stirred the sugar in his cup and gave Jean a look as if he was uncertain how she would take his next words.

"Peter, what is it?" she demanded. "Has something happened?"

1

He nodded. Suddenly there was a glint of excitement in his eyes.

"I had a letter yesterday," he said and added: "From Scotland."

"From Scotland!" she echoed, puzzled.

"It was from my grandfather," he said, looking at her over the rim of his cup.

"But you haven't got a grandfather, Peter," she exclaimed. "You told me when we met that your mother was your only relation."

She was completely bewildered. Was Peter playing some silly joke on her?

They had been engaged for nearly a year. She had a job in the typing pool of a big firm in Baston. Peter was assistant manager in a local supermarket. They had been saving desperately ever since they got engaged. They had found a house they could just afford if they both kept on working to pay the mortgage.

Peter took a letter out of his pocket and handed it over. The thick writing paper was headed with an address: Arachnock Castle, Bleiside Island, Scotland. It was dated two days before.

Dear Grandson (it read) I wish to see you. This is an urgent matter. Your mother will tell you anything you wish to know—if she has not already done so. Let me know when you will arrive and I will have the steamer met at Bleiside quay.

Your grandfather,
Angus Murray

Jean suddenly felt weak and shaky. Everything seemed suddenly to have changed. One minute she was secure, happy. Now she was not sure what this news was going to mean to Peter and her.

"And what did your mother say when you showed her the letter?" she asked, handing it back.

"I thought she would faint when she read it," he said, his good-looking face under the crisp black hair unhappy. "At first she said she didn't know anything about it. She said it must be a cruel joke someone was playing on me. But when I asked to see my father's death certificate,

3

and said I'd make enquiries on my own if she didn't help me, she broke down.

"She told me she had married my father after going on holiday to Scotland but had been terribly unhappy with him. When he had died she had brought me back to London secretly. I was only six months old at the time so I remember nothing of it, of course.

"She said she had changed our name from Murray to Henderson and my Christian name from Andrew to Peter. She got work and brought me up without telling me anything about my Scottish father. I went to school in London and later got a job. Then—I met you."

Jean could hardly believe her ears, but she had to accept that it was all very possible. She questioned Peter about his mother's romance with his father. It was a simple tale which Mrs. Henderson had told her son.

As a young woman, she had gone alone on a coach tour of Scotland. At one of the towns where the coach had stopped for a couple of hours she had gone sight-seeing

4

on her own. She went a little further than she ought to have done and suddenly realised she would miss the coach if she did not hurry back to the point where it was waiting.

In her agitation she missed her way. Breaking into a run she had dashed across a road without taking proper care. A passing car knocked her down and she finished up in hospital, though she was not badly hurt.

The next morning a good-looking Scotsman had come to see her. He had been driving the car which had knocked her down. He was carrying a bouquet of flowers. He said he was in the town on business, had called to see how she was going on, and he promised to call again the following day.

He kept his promise. He said his name was James Murray and that his family lived on a small island off the west coast. He was very handsome and charming and Ruth Chambers, as she then was, had soon found herself falling in love with him.

The upshot of it was that James Murray invited her to stay for a few days' convalescence on Bleiside Island. She was a lonely creature. She was quite alone in the world for her parents were dead. On impulse she accepted the invitation and James took her to the island when she left hospital. She met his father and sister. A week later James proposed to her and she accepted him.

"What a strange story," Jean murmured when Peter paused.

He nodded. "I find it hard to believe but my mother has convinced me it is the truth. She lived in the family home, Arachnock Castle after she married James. Apparently they didn't have a honeymoon.

"It wasn't long before she found that being married to James Murray—I still find it hard to think of him as my father! —was very different from being courted by him. He changed almost over-night, she says. His father—my grandfather, I suppose—was not pleased at the marriage and he hardly spoke to his new daughter-in-law. James' sister, Morag—my aunt—also went out of her way to make my mother unwelcome.

"James, who had seemed so much in love with Mother when they were engaged, now treated her as little better than a servant. He expected her to fetch and carry for him, drank heavily and spent a great deal of time away from her so that she was overpoweringly lonely.

"This went on for a year. I was born and, at first, Mother thought it would change my father, bring him back to the love he had lavished on her when first they met. But it didn't. He continued to go his own way and Mother wished desperately that she was safely back in London."

Peter paused. Jean said impatiently:

"What happened next? Did she run away?"

"Yes, she ran away but not just because my father was cruel to her. She ran away because he drove his car off the road when he was the worse for drink. He hit a tree and was killed instantly. That was

7

when she ran away. She had little money but she managed to get off the island and back to London with me.

"She got a job and, as I said before, brought me up single-handed. When I asked about my father as I grew older she told me he had been a seaman and had been lost in a storm. That was why there was no grave I could visit."

Jean let go a long breath. She glanced at the letter he was still holding in his hand.

"What are you going to do about that?" she asked.

His eyes narrowed as he looked at her.

"I shall visit my grandfather," he said in a low voice. "There must be a good reason why he's written to me after all this time."

"I wonder why he hasn't written to you before."

"Perhaps he did not want to. After all, he didn't evidently welcome my mother to Bleiside Island when my father married her. He was probably relieved when she ran away. Now he must have employed

8

an enquiry agency to find me. It's not a difficult thing to do if you're prepared to pay out good money."

"Will your mother want you to go?"

He shrugged. "I don't suppose so. But I must. I feel I have a duty to go. Perhaps my grandfather has something important to tell me."

She felt a sinking feeling at the pit of her stomach.

"But, Peter, what—what about us?"

He put out his hand and took hers. He smiled, a smile which showed his even white teeth and lit up his face.

"You must come with me," he said firmly. "You are the girl I'm going to marry. It's only right that my grandfather should meet you."

She bit her lip. Did she want to go to Scotland with Peter? Somehow, she thought she would rather not. She would much prefer Peter to go to Scotland on his own. He could then tell her when he returned what his grandfather was like, what he wanted with him.

Some of her doubts must have shown

in her face for Peter took her hand and pressed it.

"You must come with me, Jean," he said urgently. "I feel I want your support. All this is a bit of a mystery. I think we should face it together."

Her face cleared. She smiled.

"If you want me to go with you, Peter, of course I will," she said.

"Good girl!" He was plainly relieved. "Let's go home now and talk to Mother. You may be able to persuade her that it will be best for us to go to Bleiside Island and see my grandfather."

Peter's little car was parked nearby and they drove out to the small house where Peter and his mother had lived for many years.

It was a pleasant suburb on the fringe of London. Jean lived in digs nearby. Her mother and father were dead and she had led a rather lonely life until she had met Peter through travelling to work on the same bus every morning.

She liked Mrs. Henderson. Perhaps she

felt drawn to her because, apart from Peter, she seemed a lonely sort of person like herself.

"Mother!" Peter cried, opening the front door with his key and leading the way into the hall.

Mrs. Henderson came out of the sitting room. A glance at her face told Jean she had been crying.

"Hello, Jean," she said with an attempt at a smile.

"I told Jean everything," Peter said. "I brought her back so we could talk about the letter I had."

"You'd better both come in here," Mrs. Henderson led the way into the sitting room where a bright fire was burning.

"What do you think of the news, Jean?" the older woman asked.

"It—it was a big surprise," Jean replied.

"I suppose you think I should have told Peter the truth earlier?" Passionately she added: "But I couldn't. I was so unhappy. I just wanted to forget all about

11

the Murrays and Bleiside Island and start again. Peter was always a curious child. If I'd mentioned what happened all those years ago he would have wanted to know more. I thought it best to make a new beginning, change our name, everything!"

"I think I understand," Jean murmured.

Peter looked at his mother. There was a stubborn expression on his face.

"I'm taking Jean with me to Scotland," he said in a voice that brooked no argument. "I think it right to let my grandfather meet the girl I'm going to marry."

His mother shook her head.

"I wish you wouldn't go, Peter," she said miserably. "I'm sure it will only lead to unhappiness. You don't know what kind of a man your grandfather is. Cruel, utterly ruthless. I ought to know! I had to live with him for nearly two years."

"But he is my father's father," Peter said. "I can't just ignore his letter."

"Then write back to him and say you're not interested in going to see him."

12

"I *shall* go!" Peter said stubbornly. "And Jean has agreed to go with me."

His mother made a gesture of defeat. Her grey eyes in her thin face filled with tears.

"I can't stop you," she murmured. "But I wish you wouldn't go." Then, in a firmer tone she added, "I only hope you don't live to regret going to Bleiside Island."

"Oh, Mother, don't be melodramatic!" Peter snapped. "What could there be to regret? All I'm doing is taking the girl I'm to marry to meet an old man. Why, my grandfather must be in his seventies, at least."

"Old age doesn't always improve people," his mother said, wiping her eyes. Suddenly she exclaimed: "Hasn't it occurred to you that if your grandfather had really wanted to know something about you, he would have got in touch long before this?"

"Perhaps he's been looking for us for years."

"I don't think so, Peter," his mother

replied. "Why should he have searched for so long without results? I think it's more likely he decided to find us quite recently. I think something has happened which makes it necessary for him to get you to visit Bleiside Island. That's why I'm afraid for you."

"But if I'm his only grandson he *must* have wanted to find me years ago," Peter said, exasperated. "Any man would!"

She shook her head.

"You're not the only grandson," she said. "You remember I told you that when I first went to the Island I met your father's sister as well as his father. That sister Morag has a son—Mark—and he's older than you. When your father died your grandfather was glad to see the back of me and my child. Mark was the apple of his eye. I'm afraid your grandfather has nothing to offer you, if that's what you're thinking. Mark is heir to Arachnock Castle and most of Bleiside Island, not you."

"Perhaps Mark is dead. If so . . ."

She turned wearily away.

"That's possible, I suppose," she said. "In which case you might be his next of kin."

"Then it's more than ever necessary that I go to Bleiside Island and find out for myself," Peter said and, seeing a hard look in his grey eyes that was new to her, Jean's heart sank.

2

JEAN slept fitfully on the sleeper which had left Euston late on Monday evening for the Kyle of Lochalsh.

As the morning light strengthened round the edges of the window blind she slipped from her bunk. She pulled the edge of the blind aside and looked out at a world which brought a gasp of delight to her lips.

For the express was passing along the floor of a deep valley. Heather-clad mountains stretched to right and left. At their foot a white-capped torrent roared its way over a scattering of huge boulders.

The sun was rising and in the blue sky a cloud of seagulls swooped and dived above the fast-moving train.

Jean glanced at her wrist watch. Six o'clock! Quite some time before the express reached its destination at the

Kyle of Lochalsh, opposite the island of Skye.

There were two other passengers in the compartment: Peter and a middle-aged woman who had appeared a few minutes before the train was due to leave London. She had exchanged a few words with her fellow passengers then had wrapped herself in a voluminous cloak, climbed into her bunk and fallen asleep immediately.

Jean took her washbag out of her hold-all and, sliding the door carefully open so she would not disturb the sleepers, went along to the toilet.

A man was coming along the corridor from the other end of the train. As he stood with his back to the side so that Jean could pass, the train lurched and she found herself in his arms.

"Sorry!" she gasped, looking up into the bluest pair of eyes she had ever seen.

He grinned, a grin which transformed his rather solemn face.

"My pleasure," he said. "I see you're going to tidy up. The toilets are free. But

17

avoid the one on the left—it's not very clean."

She smiled. "Thanks!" she murmured.

Suddenly she realised that his arms were still round her. He was wearing a white tee-shirt and blue slacks. She could feel his heart beating.

"I'm sorry," he released her so suddenly that she almost fell. He grabbed her arm and steadied her.

"I think you'll feel much safer if I leave you to your own devices," he said with another smile, then headed down the corridor again.

She went into the toilet, washed and brushed her teeth. As she applied a little make-up she found herself thinking again of the main in the corridor.

About thirty, she supposed, and obviously English. There had not been a trace of Scottish accent in his deep voice.

Someone rattled the door handle and she came to with a start. She was hogging the toilet. Others wanted to freshen up as well as herself.

She went back to her compartment.

Peter was awake but the other passenger was still asleep.

"Should be there in a couple of hours," he said, climbing down from the upper bunk and giving her a kiss. "Gee, you smell nice! I'll just go along where you've been."

"You might have to wait."

But already he had the door open and had set off along the corridor in a determined fashion.

As the middle-aged lady stirred, Jean went out into the corridor again. The sun was lighting up the moor on that side of the train. Sheep were cropping contentedly. Some raised their eyes to look at the express as it flashed by, then returned to their feeding.

"Pretty desolate, isn't it?" a deep voice said at her side.

She looked into the blue eyes of the man she had spoken to in the corridor a quarter of an hour before.

"But it's very beautiful!" she said. "Very different from London."

"You live in London?" he asked.

"On the outskirts."

"This is a wonderful part of the world for a holiday," he said. "You'll enjoy yourself."

It was on the tip of her tongue to tell him that a holiday was the last thing in the world she was going on. But she didn't speak. Peter wouldn't want her mentioning their affairs to a stranger.

They stood in a companionable silence for some time, then Jean heard footsteps and looked round to see Peter approaching.

"Feel better?" she smiled.

He nodded and looked at the man by her side curiously.

"We'd better go back to our compartment," she said. "I suppose they'll serve breakfast soon."

"They'll be bringing a cup of tea round soon," the stranger said. "I doubt if you'll get any breakfast just yet."

Jean followed Peter down the corridor. As he opened the door of their compartment he asked with a frown:

"Who was that chap?"

20

She shook her head.

"I don't know," she said. "He joined me when I was looking at the scenery."

The compartment was empty. Evidently the middle-aged lady had gone to the toilet at the opposite end of the corridor.

Presently the steward appeared with cups of tea. They perched on the edge of Jean's bunk sipping the welcome hot liquid.

"I hope it's not rough on the trip over to the island," Peter said nervously.

Jean glanced through the window. There were some stunted fir trees growing along the course of the stream. Their branches were bending to a strong wind blowing off the mountains.

"It's windy," she said, then with a curious glance: "Are you afraid you might be sea-sick?"

He shrugged. "My mother used to say that I'd be sick if I had to sail across the Round Pond in Kensington Gardens," he said a trifle dolefully.

"I don't suppose it's a long trip.

Bleiside Island's just north of Skye. I found it on the map yesterday. There's a big one in the office."

She remembered the interview she had had with the supervisor of the typing pool. Miss Harris had not been too pleased to hear that one of her typists was asking for a few days' leave.

"It will have to come off your holiday later in the summer," she had said stiffly.

Jean had told Peter that she had better not be away from the office for more than three or four days or she stood a good chance of losing her job.

He had said nothing to that but she had seen from the expression on his face that he did not consider her job all that important compared with their visit to Bleiside Island.

They went to stand in the corridor until they were called to breakfast in the dining car.

There was no sign of the stranger who had talked to Jean. She was surprised to find that she felt a little disappointed by his absence.

22

The train ran into Lochalsh station on time. As they carried their zip-bags to the landing stage Peter gave the white-capped waves an uneasy look.

Jean took his hand and pressed it. She had never been sea-sick herself but she could sympathise with anyone who had.

The little steamer was waiting. It had come from Hallaig earlier and was on its daily visit to the outlying islands off the west coast.

"Perhaps you'd better go below and sit down, Peter," Jean advised, feeling the motion of the little vessel as it rose and fell to the swell.

Already his face was white. He nodded and made for an open door which led to a large cabin below.

Jean stayed on deck and drew in deep breaths of the tangy ozone. Across the narrow sound she could see the dark bulk of the Cuillin Hills on Skye and the white houses of Broadford at the back of a deep inlet. It was like being in a new world, a world of clean pure air and the fresh healthy smell of the sea.

"So you're crossing the sea to Skye," a voice said at Jean's back.

She swung round to find herself looking into the blue eyes of the man on the train.

"Oh, hello," she smiled. "No, I'm not going to Skye. My fiancé and I are going to Bleiside Island."

Just for a moment he frowned. He seemed startled by her words.

"That's a coincidence," he said. "That's where I'm going."

"Have you been before?" she asked and when he nodded: "Peter and I haven't. What's it like?"

"Quite small. Most of it's owned by a gentleman called Angus Murray. He's one of the long line of lairds who have lived at Arachnock Castle."

She smiled. "Mr. Murray is my fiancé's grandfather."

The man stared at her with interest.

"You'll hardly believe it but Arachnock Castle is my destination too," he said. "I'm Angus Murray's solicitor. I'm visiting him on business."

The little steamer was heading to the

north, leaving the long coastline of Skye away to the west. The wind was kicking up steep little white-crested waves and Jean wondered how Peter was faring in the cabin below.

"My name is Adam Simmonds," the man by Jean's side said.

"I'm Jean Clayton," Jean replied. "My fiancé's gone below. He's a poor sailor."

The solicitor looked out across the water.

"I suppose I ought to have guessed who you were," he said. "You see, Mr. Murray asked me to hire an enquiry agent to find your fiancé. His name is Peter Henderson, I believe."

"It has been most of his life," she said. "Now that he's discovered who his grandfather is I suppose he'll have to get used to being called Murray."

"He's christened Andrew Murray. I wonder if he'll want to change his name back from Peter to Andrew."

"I don't know," Jean said. "But why not ask him, for here he comes."

Peter, pale-faced, huddled in his overcoat, came towards them. Jean smiled anxiously at him.

"How do you feel?" she asked.

"Dreadful!" he replied. "But it was stuffy below. I prefer to be on deck. At least it's fresh up here."

He looked curiously at Adam Simmonds. Jean said quickly:

"Peter, this is Mr. Simmonds. He's going to Bleiside Island, too. He's your grandfather's solicitor."

Peter frowned though he took the other's outstretched hand.

"It's rather a coincidence that you're going to see my grandfather at the same time as me, isn't it?" he muttered.

"Oh, I don't really think so," the young solicitor replied. "I've just been telling your fiancée how the enquiry agent whom I employed on Mr. Murray's instructions tracked you down. Your grandfather must have asked you to visit him and then sent for me. I dare say the two events are not unconnected with each other."

"You think he might be making a

new—" Peter broke off as if he felt he had said too much.

"I think we'd better wait till we get to Arachnock Castle to find out what your grandfather's motives are in sending for us," Adam Simmonds said quietly.

He smiled at Jean, who was feeling a little embarrassed by Peter's brashness.

"And now I'll leave you to yourselves. I'm sure you have lots to talk over."

He turned and walked away along the tilting deck. Peter slipped his arm through Jean's.

"Let's find a seat in the shelter of the bridge," he said, and with a glance after the tall figure standing away towards the stern he added: "There's definitely something in the wind if my grandfather's sent for his solicitor. I wonder what it is!"

3

AN old Rolls Royce was waiting on the quayside when the little steamer drew alongside. A thin, elderly man in blue uniform was standing beside it.

"There's Duggie MacLean. He's your grandfather's chauffeur and right-hand man," Adam said as the three of them—the only passengers to disembark—went down the ramp to the quay. "He'll have come to meet us, no doubt."

As they approached the car the chauffeur saluted Adam and gave Jean and Peter a sharp look from a pair of keen dark eyes. His peaked cap, too big for him, sat on his pointed ears.

"Good morning, MacLean," the solicitor said.

"Good day to ye, Mester Simmonds!"

"This is Mr. Murray and Miss Clayton," Adam said.

28

The man opened the door at the rear of the car. Jean entered first and the two young men followed her into the musty smelling interior of the Rolls.

Jean stole a glance at Peter. It had seemed odd hearing him named Murray and not Henderson but he showed no expression. She supposed that she would have to get used to the new name. In any case, when she and Peter were married it would be her name, too!

The little village of Bleiside consisted of a score or so of white-washed cottages overlooking the sea, an inn, a couple of shops and a tiny Kirk. Several fishing boats swung at their moorings in the little harbour and a number of men in blue jerseys stared curiously at the new arrivals as Douggie MacLean got behind the wheel of the old car and drove away from the quay.

The narrow road ran parallel with the sea for a couple of miles then turned inland. The country was wild and rugged. Heather-clad moors lay at each side of the road, and the sound of rushing water could be heard above the motor as a dozen streams made their way to the sea. It was a grim, desolate landscape and Jean shivered.

"Looks like rain," Adam said and Jean looked up at the dark clouds that squatted ominously on a range of hills in the distance.

Presently the road came in sight of the sea again, this time on the west side of the island.

"There's Arachnock," Simmonds said, and looking over the chauffeur's shoulder Peter and Jean saw the battlements of a castle perched on a rocky outcrop which thrust out into the boiling sea at its foot.

It was at least a mile away and stood in silhouette against the darkening sky.

"Why, there's a farm!" Peter exclaimed, looking out of the window on his left.

Jean followed the direction of his gaze and saw a sturdy farm building over-looking the sea and surrounded by green cultivated fields.

Adam nodded. "Yes, that's the

Campbell farm. It's about the only part of Bleiside Island that doesn't belong to the Laird."

Jean saw the chauffeur's shoulders stiffen. He had heard the young solicitor's words through the opening in the glass panel which divided the front of the car from the back.

"He doesn't like the Campbells, that's plain," Jean thought; and wondered if, being loyal to his master, he hated the owner of the farm for owning a part of the island that didn't belong to the Murrays. Tribal loyalty, she guessed, was not dead in the Islands.

As the Rolls Royce swept past the low stone wall which bounded the Campbell fields a grey horse ridden by a fair-haired girl came into sight.

She was riding at a gallop, her fair hair streaming behind her. She was dressed in a shirt and breeches. She looked towards the road but did not make any move to acknowledge those in the car.

"That's Fiona Campbell," Adam said. "She's old Campbell's only child. They say her father was bitterly disappointed when she was born. He'd longed for a son to carry on the farm, which had been in the family for almost as long as the Murrays have been at Arachnock."

"Didn't he have any other children?"

"No. Fiona was the only one. His wife died a year after Fiona was born."

"Poor man," Jean murmured, looking over her shoulder through the back window.

The girl had brought the horse to a halt and was staring after the Rolls. Then suddenly, as if angry, she jerked the horse's head round and set off at a tearing gallop back the way she had come.

The Rolls proceeded along the narrow coast road and presently turned off up an even narrower track towards the castle which, perched on its crag, looked out to sea. A romantic-looking building with its towers, turrets and battlements, it had narrow slit-like windows and an arched entrance with portcullis in the square tower on the landward side.

"It's over four centuries old," Adam

Simmonds said. "The man who built it was not a very pleasant individual from all accounts. He used to prey on shipping in these parts and when anyone came to tackle him for his misdeeds he used to shut himself up in his castle until they went away. The Murray family came into possession of Arachnock in the seventeenth century."

"And they've been here ever since?" Peter murmured.

The old Rolls swept through the arched gateway into an inner courtyard. MacLean left the driving seat and came to open the door so the visitors could alight.

"Himself will be waiting for ye," he said. "Ye'll ken the way, Mr. Simmonds."

Adam nodded and looked at Peter and Jean.

"Follow me," he said and strode off across the cobbles towards a pair of stone steps which led to a door set in the high stone wall of the building.

Jean glanced at Peter. She saw him swallow and knew he was steeling himself

33

for the coming interview with his grand-father. She slipped her hand in his and he pressed it gratefully.

As they went up the steps the door was opened. A stout middle-aged woman with a cheerful, rosy face looked out at them.

"Mr. Simmonds!" she cried. "It's good to see ye, sir. The Laird is waiting for ye in his study."

She smiled at Peter, gave Jean a curious glance, then turned and led the way along a stone corridor which presently opened into a large hall whose walls were covered with tapestries depicting battle scenes and hunting incidents, mostly men hunting boar and deer with pike and sword.

A long refectory table stood in the centre of the hall and an enormous fire-place almost filled one wall. A wide stair-case led up to a balcony which ran round the hall. On these walls hung pikes and swords. At the foot of the stairs stood a full suit of armour.

"In here," the woman said and knocked on a door on the left.

Jean felt Peter tense. Now the moment had come. In a few seconds he would be face to face with the man who claimed to be his grandfather.

"Come in!" a deep voice boomed and Adam stood to one side so that Jean could go into the room first.

A man was standing with his back to the window. A pair of keen eyes in a bearded face examined the little party as the three young people went into the room.

Beyond the window Jean could hear the thunder of the sea breaking on the rocks below the castle.

The man came towards them. He had wide powerful shoulders under the jacket he wore. A kilt swung rhythmically as he moved.

"Ah, there you are, Simmonds!" he boomed.

"Good morning, Mr. Murray," Adam said, then as he turned to Jean and Peter: "I met your grandson and his fiancé on the steamer from Lochalsh."

The heavy brows came down in a

35

frown. Angus Murray said nothing as he looked, first at Peter then at Jean.

"No one told me anything about you being engaged to be married," he said at last, his eyes returning to Peter.

Peter nodded. He glanced at Jean.

"This is Jean Clayton," he said. "We're getting married in a month's time."

"Are you indeed!"

Jean could now see the lines on the craggy face, the gnarled hands. At first she had believed Angus Murray to be little more than middle-aged. Now she could see he was old, probably in his middle seventies. He carried his years well.

The piercing grey eyes under the heavy brows now looked away from Jean to his grandson.

"And you're my grandson, eh?" he said. "Yes! you're like your father, I'll say that for you. Well, welcome to Arachnock, my boy. I have much to say to you."

He looked towards the doorway where the woman was still waiting.

"Mrs. Baird will show you to your rooms." He looked over Jean's shoulder. "There'll be three rooms now, not two. See to it, woman!"

He gave Jean a look which somehow contained a mixture of curiosity and dislike then turned away.

As they went from the room she looked at Peter.

"I don't think I'm very welcome," she said in a low voice as they crossed the hall towards the staircase.

He frowned. "Nonsense! I suppose he wasn't expecting you. He'll get used to the idea of us being engaged when he's got over the initial surprise."

But his words did little to comfort her. She had a feeling that Angus Murray had a plan which did not include her. He looked the kind of man who would not let a small matter of his grandson's engagement stand in the way of any plans he had made for that grandson's future.

4

THE room into which Jean was shown had a high vaulted ceiling and two tall narrow windows which looked out towards the scattering of small islands lying like dark stains on the sea.

She could hear the tumult of the breaking waves far below. The wailing of seagulls sounded about the castle and Jean could see the birds rising and falling on the wind which moaned round the little tower in which her room was situated.

The furniture was heavy and dark. The bed was a fourposter. Thick crimson curtains hung at the windows. On the otherwise carpetless floor a thick black rug lay before the wide stone fireplace, which contained a pile of logs.

Jean put her bag on the bed and went to the dressing table to tidy her hair in the mirror.

There came a tap at the door. She

turned. This could only be Peter come to see if she was settling in all right.

"Come in," she called.

The door opened and a thin grey-haired woman in black looked in at her.

"I'm Mrs. Anderson," she said examining Jean with a great deal of interest.

Jean smiled tentatively. Who was this woman? she wondered. The housekeeper?

"Mrs. Baird tells me you are my nephew's fiancée," the other said. Her sharp-featured face did not smile. Her long bony fingers played with a gold locket which lay against her flat bosom.

"Your nephew?" Jean frowned.

"Mr. Murray is my father." She looked round the room. "I hope you are going to be comfortable. If you are cold ring and someone will come to light the fire."

She indicated a bell rope that hung on the wall, then rather abruptly she swung round and went from the room.

As Jean unpacked and put the few things she had brought with her in the drawers of a big oak chest she realised that Mrs. Anderson must be the mother of the man Peter's mother had spoken of as the heir to Arachnock.

"Mark is the heir to Arachnock Castle and most of Bleiside Island, not you," Mrs. Henderson had said.

"I wonder when we shall meet him," Jean thought, with some disquiet, for it sounded as though Mark would hardly welcome their presence.

As there was nothing else for her to do in the big gloomy room, she made for the door. She would go downstairs and find out more of this strange household to which Peter had brought her.

There was no one on the short flight of stone steps which went down from her tower room to the main passage leading to the staircase.

Reaching the hall she hesitated. Where should she go next? She knew the way to the courtyard but her main inclination was to explore that side of the castle which looked out over the sea.

Looking round she saw that another passage led off from behind the staircase and she made for it. It led her along another cold stone-flagged corridor to a small inner hall. The clatter of utensils behind a closed door on the right told her she was near the kitchen quarters of the castle. Another door tempted her and, turning the handle, she cautiously looked into the room beyond. It was a small sitting room, probably for the use of the servants, and it was empty. She closed the door and turned away.

Just as she was about to return to the main hall she noticed a narrow door in the shadow to the left. She went towards it and turned the iron handle. The door opened and she found herself looking out on a balcony which evidently ran from the back to the front of the castle. It overlooked the sea which thundered fifty feet below.

No doubt the balcony was for the use of servants who, leaving their quarters, could go round the castle wall without going through the residential part of the castle.

Jean stood at the iron railing which ran the length of the balcony.

Seagulls cried above and below her. She watched a fishing boat making for Bleiside harbour through the rough waters of the sound. The sun suddenly pierced the dark storm clouds in the east and a shaft of golden light fell across the uneasy sea.

"It's rather beautiful in a grim sort of way, isn't it?" a voice which Jean recognised sounded at her back.

Adam Simmonds laughed as she swung round.

"I'm always creeping up on you, aren't I?" he chuckled.

"I'm glad to see you," she said looking into his bright blue eyes. "I was beginning to wonder what I should do next."

"I saw you go along the passage to the stairs," he said. "When you came out here I followed."

"I had a visit from Mrs. Anderson," she said. "I suppose her son is Mr. Murray's other grandson?"

The smile died out of his eyes. His face was grave as he nodded.

"Yes, Mark Anderson is Mr. Murray's other grandson," he said.

"Is he here—at Arachnock?" she asked.

He shook his head.

"No—he's away from home at present," he replied and there was something in his voice that warned her she was touching on a subject he did not want to discuss.

She shivered suddenly. It was cold standing on the exposed balcony with a cold wind blowing in from the sea.

"We'd better go inside," he said. "Mrs. Baird told me there'd be coffee in the dining room if we wanted it."

They went down into the castle. Peter was coming downstairs as they reached the big hall.

"Hello, you two!" he exclaimed. He looked puzzled, and none too pleased.

"I went exploring," Jean said. "There's a wonderful view over the sea if you go through a door at the end of that passage."

"We were just going to have a cup of coffee," Adam said. "It's in the dining room. Follow me."

They went into a big room which at one time had probably had rough stone walls but which must have been panelled in oak more recently, Jean thought, looking round.

There was a big round table in the middle of the room and a tray with coffee pots and crockery stood on an enormous sideboard.

"Black or white?" Adam asked, crossing to the tray.

"White, please," Jean replied and Peter nodded.

"By the way, Simmonds, I'm puzzled about one thing," Peter said, taking his cup from the other man. "Where's my cousin, Mark? There seems no sign of him about the place. Is he out for the day?"

Adam frowned as he poured black coffee for himself.

"He's not on Bleiside," he said. "He's —on the mainland."

"You mean he's away—on business or holiday?" Peter asked.

44

"Not exactly. I'm not sure if it's my place to explain."

Jean looked at him curiously. What was all the mystery about?

Peter exclaimed impatiently.

"I can't understand what there is to explain. There must be some ordinary reason why he's not here at the castle."

Out of the corner of her eye Jean saw that the door was slowly opening. Whoever had turned the handle was listening outside in the hall.

When Adam did not speak Peter said, a hint of exasperation in his voice:

"Is there some reason why you can't talk about my cousin, Simmonds?"

Adam shrugged.

"I think your grandfather might have something to tell you in due course. I don't think it is for me to say anything."

The door opened suddenly. Mrs. Anderson, tense, agitated, a spot of colour in each pale cheek, confronted the three young people.

Her eyes passed from one to the other. Jean suppressed a shiver. There was

45

something strange about this woman. Her pale eyes were disturbed, the eyes of a woman at the end of her tether.

"You'll have to know sooner or later," she said in a low passionate voice. "My son is in prison!"

She pointed a trembling finger at Peter.

"That is why my father-in-law sent for you. He's going to put my poor son aside because of you. He—he—"

Her voice died away in a choking sob. Covering her thin face with one hand she pulled the door open with the other and ran from the room.

"Poor woman!" Adam said, and crossing the door to close it: "Mark was mixed up in some drug smuggling. He was sent to prison for eighteen months. Come to think of it, he must be due for release fairly soon. I think personally he was more sinned against than sinning. I believe the people he went about with were the real culprits. Mark didn't realise what was going on until it was too late."

"Did you have something to do with the court case?" Jean asked.

"Yes, as Mr. Murray's solicitor I organised his grandson's defence. We had an extremely good barrister who got Mark a comparatively light sentence. That's something to be thankful for, I suppose. But of course his grandfather can only see one side of it: the disgrace to an ancient family. He might have forgiven Mark for getting mixed up with the wrong people —but he'll never forgive him for dragging the family name in the mud. There was a great deal in the papers at the time."

He looked at Peter.

"So now you can understand why your grandfather sent for you to come to Arachnock."

"You mean, he's going to make me his heir, not my cousin?"

Adam shrugged.

"I'd rather leave him to explain things to you," he said with a frown. "I've already said more than I should."

Jean looked from one young man to the other. With every moment that passed it was becoming clearer why Adam Simmonds had been summoned to

Arachnock at the same time as Peter. As Mr. Murray's solicitor he was there to make another will naming her fiancé as heir to the estate. It would be a very difficult existence from the one they had planned together until this moment. She looked at Peter, and noticed the suppressed satisfaction in his face. It disquieted her. From Angus Murray's reception of her short time before, she wondered if there was a future for her at Arachnock Castle.

5

THE old man looked at Adam across the wide desk. He was scowling as he ran his fingers through his tangled beard.

"You didn't tell me—after you had found my grandson that he was engaged to be married to this girl he's brought with him," he said angrily.

"The enquiry agent I used to find your grandson said nothing about Miss Clayton in his report, sir," Adam said.

Mr. Murray thrust back his chair and began to pace up and down the room.

"My grandson can't marry that girl!" he snapped at last, swinging round to glare at the solicitor.

"But he's engaged to her," the other protested.

"Then he must get un-engaged! Damn it, man, you know what I have in mind. If Mark hadn't disgraced us all there would have been no call even to find Andrew. He and Fiona were in love. They would have married and I would have had the Campbell land which would have been added to the Murrays. Then I'd really have owned Bleiside Island!"

There was a frustrated gleam in the old eyes under the shaggy brows. Adam said nothing.

He knew that this had been the old man's dream for many years—to own the whole of the island, to add the Campbell farm and its surrounding fields to his own considerable estate. True enough, if Fiona Campbell had married Mark the Campbell acres would—when Mr. Campbell died—have fallen like a ripe plum into the Laird of Arachnock's lap.

"You sent for me so that I would draw up a new will, I take it?" he said.

The old man resumed his pacing. He went to the window and looked out over the sea, leaden under the gathering storm clouds.

"We'll leave the matter of a new will until I've had a talk to my grandson," he muttered. "If he can't be persuaded to change his mind about marrying this girl the whole purpose of bringing him here will be lost."

Adam frowned at the old man's back. What a strange family this was. A grandson in prison, the old man's daughter mentally disturbed because of her son's escapade, the head of the family obsessed by illusions of grandeur, and supposing that he could arrange a marriage of convenience as if he were some medieval lord.

Adam found himself wishing he hadn't inherited the Laird of Arachnock as a client when his father had died a year before. He foresaw squalls ahead and however he looked at it, the likely outcome looked ominous.

He felt sorry for Jean Clayton, who had been dragged into a situation she could never have anticipated when she had promised to marry the man she was in love with. From what he had seen of Peter—Andrew as old Angus Murray insisted on calling him, he could not help wondering whether avarice might not prove more powerful than love. Jean was likely to be hurt, and hurt badly, Adam thought, and his heart filled with pity for her.

For even if the man she loved insisted on rejecting his grandfather's plans for him, and they returned to London and married according to plan, she would always feel guilty that she had prevented her husband from coming into a rich inheritance which could have been his for the asking.

He was conscious that Angus Murray had turned from the window and was staring at him questioningly.

"What do you think my grandson's reaction will be when I suggest he sends this English girl away and settles here at Arachnock Castle as my heir?" the old man asked.

"It depends how much he cares for her," Adam replied.

"You mean he might defy me and go ahead and marry this girl—in spite of everything?" There was menace in the old voice now.

"There is no reason to suppose he will not keep his promise. After all, it would be hard to cast her off like an old coat when he's asked her to be his wife."

The old man crashed one big fist into the palm of his other hand.

"Damn it, man, whose side are you on?" he roared.

"You asked me a question, sir, and I gave you an answer based on a reasoned view of the situation," Adam said coldly.

Mr. Murray regarded him for a few seconds with a stony stare. Then he made a gesture of dismissal.

"All right, Simmonds," he said. "You'd better send my grandson in and I'll have a talk to him. The sooner I find out more about him the better."

Adam turned and went from the room. He found Jean and her fiancé in the library, a big room at the back of the house.

A log fire was burning in the open fireplace. Books lined two of the walls.

The rain which had threatened earlier was now beating against the high windows, but the comfortable sofa and deep armchairs ranged about the fireplace gave the room a cosy, lived-in look. Adam smiled at the young couple, who had turned to look at him as he came into the room, and he felt a little more comfortable than he had felt in Angus Murray's study. The library was the only room in the castle where he ever felt at home.

"Your grandfather wants to talk to you, Andrew . . . er, Peter," he said. "He's waiting in his study."

The young man scrambled up from the sofa.

"I'd better go to him," he said. "He doesn't seem the kind of chap to take kindly to being kept waiting."

Adam grinned. "You've got something there! The study is across the hall."

"I still can't get used to being called Andrew. I suppose I'll have to, though, as it's the name I was given when I was christened."

"We've been talking to Mrs. Baird,"

Jean said. "She remembers Peter being christened at the little church in Bleiside. She was only a girl at the time."

"I suppose she remembers his mother, then?" Adam said after Andrew had hurried from the room.

"She says she was very pretty. Mrs. Baird lived in the village and only came to work here at the castle ten years ago."

"She wouldn't know Andrew's father?"

"She knew him by sight. She said he was very handsome and she could understand an impressionable young girl falling for him. Apparently he had quite a reputation locally."

"Wine, women and song?"

"Something like that," Jean smiled.

She looked into the flames of the fire. The smile had gone from her face now.

"I don't think Peter's—I mean Andrew's—grandfather is too pleased to find that his grandson is engaged. He didn't say anything to me at lunch time. I met his eyes once and they didn't look particularly friendly."

Poor girl! Adam thought. I wonder

what she'd say if I told her what had just passed between old Murray and me.

He felt a sudden impulse to sit beside her on the sofa and comfort her. But he resisted it.

It was too early for her to learn that the Laird bitterly resented her appearance at Arachnock Castle. Although he had not known her long, he had a feeling that she was a proud girl and that she would never stay a moment longer than she had to in a place where she was not wanted.

Perhaps young Murray would stand up to his grandfather and convince him that it would, in the end, be the best for all parties if he married the girl he loved.

A sudden feeling of loneliness overwhelmed him. What a lucky fellow Andrew Murray was.

He looked down at the soft golden-brown hair of the girl, gazed into her hazel eyes as she smiled up at him, and compared his own life with Andrew's.

He was a bachelor and had a set of rooms in the West End of London. A competent housekeeper looked after him.

He had a prosperous practice and plenty of friends. But he had never been in love. Girl friends—he'd had a few of those. But he had never felt any desire to spend the rest of his life with any one of them.

Sometimes he thought that the best things in life were pasing him by. A wife, a home of his own, children . . .

I'm thirty-one, he thought. A stodgy, stuffy solicitor. I've never felt I'll be anything else until—today.

Jean, meeting his eyes, wondered what he was thinking. He was nice. She had liked him from the moment she had met him when she had more or less fallen into his arms in the corridor of the express from London. She felt she needed a friend badly. In this man she believed she had found one.

She looked away and back to the fire.

"I suppose Mrs. Murray must be very upset because her son went to prison," she said.

He nodded. "Yes, it was a terrible blow to her. She adores Mark. In fact, it was such a shock at the time that she became ill. She went across to the mainland for a while."

"You mean, to a hospital?"

He frowned. Had he said too much? But this girl ought to know the true state of things at the castle.

"It was a special kind of nursing home," he said in a low voice. "Mrs. Anderson had a nervous breakdown. She only came back to Arachnock a short time ago."

"Poor woman," Jean murmured. "It must be dreadful living here with an old man who hates his own grandson—her son. I suppose a mother will always love her son, whatever he has done."

"It would perhaps have helped her if she had had the support of her husband. But he died some eight years ago when Mark was still away at school."

She swung round and looked up at him from her seat on the sofa.

"Mr. Simmonds, what do you think Mr. Murray will ask of my fiancé? Somehow, I can't help thinking he's not over-enthusiastic about Andrew and me getting married."

Adam forced a hypocritical smile.

"I shouldn't worry your head about that. If Andrew loves you he'll marry you whatever his grandfather says."

She shook her head somewhat sadly.

"I wish I agreed with you, but I don't. Mr. Murray seems a strong, stubborn man. If he makes Andrew his heir he'll expect something in return. And that could mean breaking our engagement and sending me back to London. Peter would love to be rich—a landowner. It would be hard for him to resist."

"You mustn't think on those lines."

"But, Mr. Simmonds!—"

"Couldn't you call me Adam?" he asked and went round the end of the sofa to stand by her side. "If you're in love with Andrew and he's in love with you, a crabby old man isn't going to say whether or not the two of you should get married." Adam did not feel as confident as he sounded.

Tears filled her eyes.

"I feel so helpless, somehow," she whispered. "I'm so far from everything I know and understand. I—I—"

She broke off because she was afraid she would break down and disgrace herself.

He put out his hands and gripped her arms just above the elbows. Sudden tenderness swept over him. He remembered how she had lain against him in the train, her softness, her scent stirring his senses.

"Jean, it's too early to upset yourself," he murmured. "Why, at this very moment Andrew's probably telling his grandfather how much he loves you and how he means to marry you whatever the Laird says."

She looked up at him, eyes swimming, soft lips trembling.

"Thank you for being so kind— Adam," she whispered. "I'll always be grateful to you."

He drew her closer. A sudden madness seized him. Her mouth was within inches of his own.

A moment later he would have kissed her; then there came a knock at the door and he stepped back.

Mrs. Blair put her rosy, smiling face around the door.

"I've taken a pot of tea into the study for the Laird and young Mr. Murray," she said. "Would you like a cup in here, miss?"

Jean forced a smile and hoped that, as she had her back to the rain-lashed window the woman would not see her tears.

"Thank you, Mrs. Blair, that would be very nice," she said.

"I baked one of my special sponge cakes this morning, Mr. Simmonds," the other said. "I know you have a fancy for it so I'll bring it in."

"Yes indeed, Mrs. Blair, how splendid!"

She disappeared. Jean met Adam's eyes. Simultaneously they burst out laughing.

6

"YOU'RE like your father, lad!" There was an almost tender gleam in the old grey eyes looking up at the young man standing in front of Angus Murray's desk.

"I wouldn't know that, sir." Andrew's voice was stiff. "My mother never showed me any photographs of him."

"Then I will," the old man said and opened a drawer at his side.

Andrew, taking the likeness in his own hand, looked down at the photograph of his father. He saw a dark-haired young man with twinkling eyes and a small moustache above a laughing mouth. He was dressed in plaid and kilt and had a glengarry worn at a rakish angle on his head.

"I suppose your mother told you she ran away," the Laird said, returning the photograph to the drawer.

"Yes, and she told me why!" Andrew said sharply. "I gather she wasn't made very welcome on Bleiside Island from the start, and that my father ill-treated her the whole time she lived here at the castle with him. No wonder she went back to London when he was killed."

For a moment the old man's face darkened. His grey eyes filled with pain.

"It was a great tragedy, a great tragedy, indeed," he muttered.

"Who for? You or my mother?" Andrew asked, a defiant note in his voice.

The old man shrugged his wide shoulders as if to shake off a load of painful memories.

"I can understand you being bitter, lad," he said. "No doubt your mother has painted both your father and me in the blackest colours. But she forgets that at first she was happy, and even though I never approved of Fergus marrying her I did not hold their marriage against her. Fergus was wild—I'll grant you that— but I'm sure at heart he loved his wee English lassie."

"He didn't treat her as if he did!"

Angus Murray sighed. "Maybe not," he agreed. "Let's not drag up the past, lad. What I want to do now is talk about the future."

"But I have a future, sir. I have a good job in London, I'm getting married—"

"Stop!" The old man raised his hand. His eyes flashed. "The future of a shop assistant and the future of the heir to an ancient family name are two very different things."

"I'm not a shop assistant!" Andrew cried indignantly. "I'm an assistant manager. In time I'll be promoted. There's a big future in my line of business."

"Supermarkets!" The old voice was a sneer now. "For God's sake, lad, where's your sense of priorities? We're talking about an ancient name, a large estate, a great deal of money. If I make you my heir you'll be one of the most important men in the Isles."

Andrew was silent. He stared across the

desk at the old man and some of the resentment had gone from his eyes now.

"I own the whole of Bleiside Island," the Laird said. "All but a small portion which will be mine in the end. Everybody on the island works for me—the fishermen, the crofters, even the road workers. There's just one man who's stupid enough to defy me."

"Mr. Campbell?" Andrew said softly.

The grey eyes glared up at him.

"What do you know about Stuart Campbell?" he demanded.

"We passed his farm on the way from the village. Mr. Simmonds pointed it out."

"Campbells have been at Bannock Farm for a very long time—I'll grant you that," the Laird said. "But Campbell's an ailing man who is heavily in debt. If he had any sense he'd sell his land to me and retire to the mainland. There's no son to follow him."

"Only a daughter."

"Aye, there's a daughter. She and Mark—but never mind that! I mean to have Campbell's land to add to mine. It's only a matter of biding my time. Campbell will die. As for his daughter—well!"

The gnarled fingers tapped on the polished top of the desk. There was a red glint in the grey eyes under the lowering brows.

"He's crazy," Andrew thought. "These Campbells have defied him for so long that he thinks of nothing else."

Angus Murray raised his eyes and looked into his grandson's face again. He was calmer now.

"I'm going to make you my heir, Andrew," he said slowly. "That's why I sent for Simmonds. I shall be making a new will and he'll take it back to London with him."

"But—isn't your other grandson older than me? Surely he should be your heir."

The colour faded from the old man's face. He crashed his fist on to the desk.

"Don't speak of him!" he cried. "He has dishonoured the name of a family that has never known a scandal before. I have disowned him. You know where he is?"

"Simmonds told me."

"Then you'll know why I am making a new will. Oh, they made excuses for Mark at the time. But nothing can excuse the fact that he disgraced himself and me. I have finished with him. I never want to see him again."

"So you're going to settle for second-best—me?" There was a hint of sarcasm in Andrew's voice.

"I'm settling for you, as you term it, because you are the only grandson I have. My son died; I was left with a daughter."

The Laird's voice was bitter.

"You mean Mark's mother; my aunt, I suppose she is?" Andrew said quietly.

The other did not seem to hear him. He asked:

"What about this girl you've brought with you from England?" he demanded.

"My fiancée, the girl I'm going to marry?"

The old man eyed him in silence for

nearly half a minute. He appeared to be considering his next words carefully.

"The wife of the Laird of Arachnock holds a very responsible position, boy," he said at last. "Your father made a sad mistake when he brought your mother to the island. I don't want you to do the same thing."

"Are you suggesting that I send Jean away?" Andrew demanded angrily.

"I suggest you think things over very carefully before you commit yourself irrevocably to something you may regret all your life."

"But I love Jean! We're to be married in less than a month."

"I tell you she will not do—not here, at the Castle. Can you not see that?" Angus Murray paused, but Andrew said nothing, and he went on:

"You must choose. Either you become heir to a fortune and the ownership of Bleiside Island—or you go back to your damned shop wherever it is, and live in a semi-detached villa in some grubby suburb."

When the young man still did not speak his grandfather said in a kinder voice.

"She's a very pretty lass, I'll grant you that, lad. But she won't be accepted by the people of Bleiside Island, not as the wife of the Laird of Arachnock Castle."

Andrew looked into the deep-set eyes in the wrinkled bearded face, prepared to make an angry response. He would tell this old monster that he had no intention of giving up Jean, that he would return with her to England immediately, that he had no interest in inheriting the position of his disgraced cousin.

But something held him back. Perhaps, as the old man had suggested, he ought to think things over before acting impulsively. There was no point in antagonising his grandfather. Perhaps when his grandfather saw what a sweet, intelligent girl Jean was he would change his mind and accept her as the wife of the man who was to succeed him as Laird of Arachnock.

And if he, the Laird, accepted her, the people of Bleiside Island would follow suit. At any rate, it would be silly to squander the chance of a fortune for the sake of an outburst of chivalrous anger.

He looked at the old man sitting watchfully behind the big desk. Surely he could not expect him to throw over his engagement just like that?

Why, if he let the Laird make him his heir, he too would sit at that desk, he too would rule this little island. No more pinching and scraping; no more wondering if he and Jean would be able to keep up the payments on the mortgage they would have to raise to buy a house to live in; no more wondering if at any time he might be made redundant and have to worry about where the next penny was coming from.

Yes! The whole thing needed carefully thinking over.

He must go to Jean and ask her what she thought. That was the only fair thing to do.

He turned and made for the door. Before he left the room, he looked back at the man watching him from behind the desk.

"Give me twenty-four hours," he said. "Then I'll come and talk to you again."

The old man nodded. As the door closed behind Andrew he stroked his beard.

A chuckle rose in his throat.

"The way to catch a salmon is to offer it something attractive and let it hook itself," he thought. "I think I've got that young man firmly hooked. Now I've only to draw him to the gaff."

7

ANDREW found Jean with Adam
Simmonds—again, had he
nothing else to do?—before the
fire in the library. A tray stood on a small
table in front of Jean. She was pouring
Adam a second cup of tea as Andrew
came into the room.

"Peter, come and have a cup of tea,"
she cried.

He frowned. "You'll have to get used
to calling me Andrew, Jean," he said, "at
least while we're here."

"I'm sorry," she said, handing him a
steaming cup. "I've always known you as
'Peter'. In time I suppose I'll be calling
you 'Andrew' naturally enough, but it still
seems a bit strange."

It flashed across his mind that she
might not call him anything if he agreed
to his grandfather's terms. Then he put
the disloyal thought aside.

He loved Jean, didn't he? He must get his grandfather to change his mind about her. Surely he would when he saw how much they meant to each other, he and Jean. He remembered once telling her that he couldn't imagine life without her. Of course, that was down south. Circumstances were different here, very different. You had to admit that.

Adam got up from one of the big armchairs. He put his cup on the tray.

"I'll leave you two together," he said. "I have some business to discuss with the Laird and this seems an opportune moment to do it."

He gave them a smile and made for the door. When he had gone from the room Jean smiled at Andrew.

"Come and sit down and tell me what your grandfather had to say," she said.

He sank down on to the sofa by her side. As he sipped his tea he stared moodily at the fire.

"He's a strange old man," he muttered. "I don't know how to take him."

"Did he talk about—us?" she asked quietly.

He nodded. "Yes. He seemed to think history was repeating itself."

She frowned. "You mean, you bringing me here as your father brought your mother to Bleiside Island?"

"Something like that," he admitted.

"So he's against our engagement?"

"Why do you think that?"

"Because he was against your father marrying your mother. He must feel the same way about me. I suppose he has someone else in mind for you if you're to be his heir and the Laird of Arachnock."

He put his cup down and looked at her. That was a possibility that hadn't occurred to him.

"But who on earth could he have in mind for me on Bleiside Island?"

"There may be half a dozen eligible girls, for all we know. After all, we've only been here a few hours.'

"I think you're letting your imagination run away with you, Jean," he said rather crossly. "In any case, I told him you were the girl I loved and that we were going to get married."

The word "were" gave Jean an unpleasant jolt. Wouldn't it have been more natural to say "we *are* going to get married".

"What did he say to that?" she asked.

"He wasn't too pleased, I must admit. He rambled on with some nonsense about the wife of the Laird of Arachnock holding a very responsible position. He said I had to decide whether I wanted to be his heir—or return to London and forget all about Arachnock Castle and Bleiside Island."

"And what was your reply?" Jean asked quietly.

"Nothing! I just walked out on him," the young man said, and wondered if Jean believed him.

She bit her lip.

"So when do we go back to London?" she asked, and she could feel her heart bumping unpleasantly in her breast as she waited for his reply.

He put his hand over hers.

"There's nothing to be gained by rushing back to London like a couple of spoilt children," he said. "We must stay, at least for a little while, so that you can get to know my grandfather better. I'm sure he'll grow to love you, as I love you, when he sees what a marvellous girl you are."

"He never grew to love your mother," she murmured.

He did not reply to that, just got up and walked over to the window and looked out. The rain had stopped and a shaft of sunlight had pierced the clouds to fall like a silver pathway across the dark sea.

"It's a beautiful place," he said turning back to Jean. "Let's go for a walk, we have a lot of exploring to do."

With more apparent enthusiasm than she felt, Jean jumped up. It would be good to have some exercise. Much better than sitting here speculating on an uncertain future.

"I'll go up and get my coat," she said and hurried from the library.

Up in her room she stared for sometime into the dressing-table mirror.

What did Andrew really want to do: become his grandfather's heir—or return to London and marry her? There was a vast difference between being the heir of a rich man, future laird of a Socttish estate, and being the assistant manager of a provincial supermarket!

She had swiftly sensed that there were doubts in the mind of the man who had asked her to marry him so short a time ago. She wondered now if Peter—Andrew—had ever really loved her. Could he change his feelings as easily as he changed his name?

But doubts were no good to her. She wanted a complete commitment on her man's part. There could be no half measures.

Either he must break their engagement, and let her go home at once, or he must tell his grandfather that love meant more to him than all the money and position in the world. Somehow, she did not feel that old Angus Murray would easily change his attitude towards her.

With a sigh she pulled on her coat and went downstairs again.

They left the castle by the door which led into the courtyard. As they went down to the shore road the wind blowing off the sea almost took their breath away. They walked slowly along the road down which they had come that morning in the Rolls Royce.

"While you were with your grandfather I was talking to Adam," Jean said, hands deep in the pockets of her coat for the wind was cold.

He gave her a sharp look. She wondered if he didn't like her calling his grandfather's solicitor by his first name after such short acquaintance. Surely he didn't think she and Adam . . . To her own surprise, she felt a twinge of guilt. Adam *was* attractive.

"Well?" Andrew said brusquely.

"He told me something about your aunt. Apparently when her son went to prison she had a nervous breakdown. She was in a nursing home for some weeks. She only came back to the castle a short while ago."

He nodded. "She does seem to be a strange woman. I suppose the shock of her son turning out to be mixed up with drugs must have been a severe one."

After a few more paces he said:

"I suppose she must hate me. My coming here to take her son's place as my grandfather's possible heir will have been a bitter blow."

"I dare say she'd be delighted if we went back to England and left the field clear for your cousin again. Your grandfather may be an unforgiving man, but he must leave the estate to someone."

He nodded but said nothing more on the subject. As they walked along the road with the bleak moorland on one side and the sea with a distant view of the islands in the sound on the other, Jean suddenly exclaimed.

"There's just one thing your grandfather has forgotten when he had talked to you about making you his heir."

79

He looked at her, puzzled.

"What's that?" he asked.

"He evidently hasn't asked you if I would enjoy coming to live on Bleiside Island—as your wife."

He frowned. "But I suppose he assumed, if I agreed to follow him here at Arachnock Castle, that you'd come as well. That is, if he realised that giving us his blessing was the only way to get me to live in the castle."

"And why should he assume that?" she demanded, hazel eyes flashing.

"Well, you—you'd be my wife. Naturally, I'd expect you to—" He broke off.

"You expect that I'd fall in with your grandfather's wishes, uproot myself from everything I know and take my place by your side—just because you fell in with your grandfather's wishes and allowed him to make you his heir!"

"But I haven't told him I'll agree to be his heir! I told him I loved you and—"

Jean's indignation was only partly assumed. She wanted to provoke Andrew

80

into being frank about his plans, but she was also angry that neither he nor his grandfather had given much thought to her own wishes.

"You told him you'd think it over, didn't you? You didn't say outright that you loved me and that we were going back to London and getting married in a few weeks. Full stop!"

"Well, yes, I suppose I did say something like that," Andrew admitted. "After all, this is a very serious matter."

"Going back home, getting married to me, and forgetting all about your grandfather's offer and Arachnock Castle is a serious matter, too, Peter. You don't seem to realise that."

He was looking distressed, but she went on, "No Peter, you've got to make your mind up. Dithering isn't any good. Either you want to be your grandfather's heir—or you want to marry me. Which is it to be?"

"You're unreasonable, Jean," he complained, and his face took on a cold, disapproving expression as he turned to look at her. "You treat the whole situation as if it didn't matter at all."

"And to you it's the biggest thing that ever happened in your life! Is that it?"

"You must admit it's the biggest thing that is ever likely to happen to either of us. Heir to a rich man, owner of Arachnock Castle—and all this!"

He looked round him and there was something in his face that sent a shiver through her. She had never thought of him as a very ambitious person. But she could see that he was excited by the idea of himself as a Scottish Laird.

Whatever he might say about her happiness coming first, he couldn't hide from her that the thought of becoming a rich man's heir was hugely—perhaps irresistibly—attractive to him.

She stopped in the middle of the narrow road and looked up at him. There was a determined set to her chin and a glint in her large eyes.

"Peter, you've got to make up your mind one way or the other," she said in a firm but unhappy voice. "You know how I feel. Now you must choose between a life here on Bleiside Island—or a life as my husband in much less attractive circumstances."

"But I'd be your husband if we married and I became my grandfather's heir," he said, more than a hint of exasperation in his voice.

In despair she said:

"You still don't understand, Peter!"

He frowned at her.

"Why can't you call me by my real name?" he demanded. "It's Andrew— Andrew Murray. I stopped being Peter Henderson when my grandfather's letter came."

His extraordinary willingness to adopt his grandfather's family name seemed to Jean a sign of his true desires. Tears filled her eyes. She turned away and stared out to sea.

If only she could be as happy as she had been two days before. Now everything had changed. Something told her that not only her happiness, but Peter's happiness too, was in danger.

They must get away from Bleiside Island without delay, or Peter never would. She remembered something Peter's mother had said the day Peter had shown him his grandfather's letter:

"I only hope you don't live to regret going to Bleiside Island."

She heard footsteps and looked round. Peter was striding off down the road, head hunched inside the collar of his coat. The whole movement of his body indicated irritation and indecision. He did not look back when she called after him.

After a few seconds watching him stride away she turned and made back the way they had come.

Better to leave him to his thoughts for a while. Maybe then he would begin to see things her way.

She hardly noticed she had reached the castle until she was confronted by the slope up to the arched entrance which led into the courtyard.

She halted. Did she want to go back into the castle? The thought of sitting by herself thinking of the argument she had just had with Peter did not appeal.

She looked round.

She noticed that there was a gap in the wall which ran alongside the shore. She decided that a brisk walk beside the sea would be better than moping in the library.

She went through the narrow opening and found herself on a sandy beach. This ran alongside the spur of land on which Arachnock Castle had been built hundreds of years before.

She could see the white caps of waves breaking on the point where the land met the sea. She decided she would walk as far as she could then turn and go back to the castle by way of the main gate.

The fresh cold wind off the sea was exhilarating. A little of the depression she had felt when Peter—she still found it hard to think of him by any other name —had gone striding off on his own, was blown away with the breeze.

She walked briskly over the sand

drawing in deep breaths of the pure ozone-filled air.

Suddenly she thought:

"Perhaps I'm being unfair to Peter. Perhaps I ought to consider if I really would be unhappy on Bleiside Island. After all, if I love Peter and want to marry him I should be prepared to live in the home he provides for me, wherever it happens to be."

Then her thoughts once more changed directions.

"It's just that something warns me about giving in too tamely. By holding out I'll probably persuade Peter to go back to his natural environment— our natural environment—in a modest English suburb. It's where we were brought up, the kind of background which is natural to both. Surely we would, each of us, be out of place in a remote Scottish Castle.

She reached the end of the sandy beach. She stood looking at the waves dashing against the rocks below the castle. The rocks formed a not very formidable barrier between the sandy beach on which she stood and whatever lay beyond, presumably another stretch of beach.

Surely it would be easy to scramble over the rocks and see what was on the other side.

A moment later she was making her way between the first of the rocks that barred her path, the spray from the waves chill on her face. Five minutes later she reached the topmost rock and found herself looking into an attractive sandy cove backed by a precipitous cliff. A quarter of a mile away another barrier of rocks barred the way and this obstacle was already almost covered by waves.

She decided she would walk across the cove then turn and return the way she had come.

Carefully she found her way through the rocks, the spent waves lapping at her feet, and was soon standing on the beach below.

What a heavenly little cove, she

thought as she made her leisurely way under the cliff towards the almost submerged rocks at the far end.

It would be a wonderful place to bathe on a hot sunny day. Whoever used it would have it entirely to themselves.

When she reached the rocks she sat for a while looking out to sea. She found herself thinking, not of the man she was to marry, but of Adam Simmonds who had come into their lives only a few hours ago. She wondered what he thought of his client making a stranger—for that was what Peter was to the Laird—his heir. Adam had given no hint of his own thoughts about the curious situation in which she and Peter were placed.

Did he think Peter ought to fall in with the old man's wishes; or that he should go back to London and resume his life there?

After a while, she sighed and got to her feet and started back towards the rocks over which she must scramble to reach the entrance to the castle.

She soon reached them. But to her

dismay she found that they were almost covered by the incoming tide. Now the waves that had not quite reached the cliff on which the castle stood had covered all the rocks.

As she watched a huge wave, white-capped, came rolling in from the sound. Holding her breath she saw it sweep over the top of the rocks which had been uncovered when she had crossed them half an hour before.

It dashed itself against the cliff with a great roar.

When she had climbed down into the cove she had not thought to wonder whether the tide was coming in or going out. Now she was trapped. If she tried to cross the rock barrier, she would be swept into the sea by the next big wave. She was a prisoner in the little cove which had seemed so attractive a few moments before.

Then, the full extent of her predicament struck her with horrid force. In a little while, perhaps half an hour if the tide continued at its present rate, the cove itself would be under water! With sudden fear she looked up at the sheer cliff face towering up from the beach.

8

ANDREW MURRAY strode off down the road, hands deep in the pockets of his coat, head thrust a little forward. His eyes were angry; his mouth tight and stubborn.

He was angry with Jean. Why couldn't she have been more understanding of the predicament he found himself in? It was all very well talking about returning to London without giving his grandfather's offer to make him his heir another thought.

He looked round at the wide expanse of moorland, at the distant hills, at the sandy beach up which the tide was creeping.

All this could be his. All he had to do was say "Yes!" to his grandfather's proposal. Of course there were complications. Jean, for instance.

His grandfather was against him marrying her at present.

But Angus Murray was an old man. Rather than see his grandson disappear back to London, never to be seen again, he would surely come to accept Jean as his heir's wife. It would just take a little time to win him over.

There seemed to be no real reason why he shouldn't come round. It wasn't as if being married to Jean would actually prevent him becoming his grandfather's heir, if the old man could be persuaded. Jean was attractive, young, sensible. She hadn't been brought up to become the wife of a rich man, but he wasn't used to the idea of belonging to the landed gentry either.

He looked up suddenly at the thunder of hoofs.

To his amazement a horse was galloping towards him. It was a grey and its mane was waving in the wind as it careered down the road.

It was obviously badly frightened. Something had scared it and it had bolted, probably throwing its rider at the same time.

"Whoa!"

Andrew threw himself to one side.

The road was very narrow, bounded by low stone walls, and there was little room to pass.

As the horse drew abreast of him, reins swinging free, he grabbed at them without thinking of the possible disastrous consequences.

The horse checked for a moment, then as Andrew took a firm grip on the reins, it went on its way.

The young man felt as if his right arm had been wrenched from its socket. But he held on, and after a few yards the horse came to a halt trembling violently.

"There, there! It's all right! Calm down!"

Andrew hardly recognised his voice as he attempted to soothe the animal. His action had been purely instinctive. Now he felt amazed that he had risked his life like that. One slip and he would have been under the plunging hoofs.

"Thank God you caught him! He might have tried to jump the wall and could have ended up with a broken leg."

It was a girl's voice. Andrew found himself looking into a pair of green eyes in a white scared face. The girl's fair hair was blowing loose about her slim shoulders.

"He threw me when a rabbit jumped out of the wall right under his feet," she said. "I'm lucky to be all in one piece. I ought by rights to have broken my neck!"

She walked slowly up to the horse and patted it. It turned its head and gave her what seemed to Andrew an apologetic look.

"You're a bad boy, Prince," the girl's soft voice said. She looked at Andrew and there was a faint smile on her red lips. "I suppose you think I should be cross with him. But it wasn't really his fault."

He smiled back at her. He knew who she was now. He had seen her riding this very horse as he rode in the Rolls Royce with Jean and Adam Simmonds, after they had landed on the island.

"You're Fiona Campbell, aren't you?" he said.

She laughed. "And you're the Laird's grandson just arrived from the South."

"How do you know that?"

"I saw you in the back of the Laird's car. In any case, everyone on the island knows you've arrived. This is a small community, Mr. Murray. Everyone knows everyone else's business."

She picked up the trailing reins. He noticed as she turned the horse that she was limping.

"You did hurt yourself when you were thrown!" he exclaimed.

"It's nothing," she said a trifle impatiently. "I'll be as right as rain after a hot bath."

She made as if to put her foot up to the stirrup to mount then winced.

"Perhaps I'll walk him back," she said, reluctantly.

"May I walk with you? I came out for a stroll."

"I can't stop you," she said and the

green eyes twinkled up at him as he fell in by her side.

"I gather that your father and my grandfather are at loggerheads," he said as they walked slowly along the road.

She frowned. "The Laird can't bear to think that another man might own an acre or two of his precious Bleiside Island. But he forgets that Campbells have been on Bleiside almost as long as Murrays."

"I only met my grandfather for the first time today. He struck me as being a man who would never give up a fight for something he had set his heart on."

She nodded. "My father's the same, though—"

Sudden sadness clouded the green eyes.

"Daddy's a sick man," she said. "And the Laird knows that. I suppose he thinks he'll wear him down in the end. It might have been different if he'd had a son to take the Laird on. But—well, he only has me."

"I'm sure you're a fighter."

She shrugged.

"It might have been different if—" She broke off.

He frowned. "If—what?" he asked gently.

She faced him and now her eyes were flashing.

"I'm engaged to your cousin, Mark," she said in a low angry voice. "But Mark's across there"—she glanced for a moment at the sea—"and his grandfather has disowned him."

He said nothing to this. So this girl and his cousin must have got engaged before Mark was arrested and sent to prison.

He wondered if she still loved the man who had disgraced an ancient name.

She looked sideways at him.

"You have heard of—Mark's trouble?" she asked.

He nodded. "My grandfather told me. He thinks Mark let him—the family—down."

"I suppose he's right. Angus Murray is a very proud man. The thought of what Mark did would be a heavy blow for him to take."

"And you'll go away from Bleiside Island when my cousin's free?"

"What makes you think I'd still be willing to marry Mark when he comes out of prison?" she asked sharply. "It was as much a shock to me when he was sent to prison as it must have been to his grandfather."

For some reason he felt pleased at her words. He wondered why. She meant nothing to him.

"When will Mark be free?" he asked.

"Some months yet."

"But you won't marry him?"

"I'm not sure." She gave him an angry look. "In any case, it's got nothing to do with you. There was a very pretty girl riding in the back of the Laird's car with you. You should be more concerned with her than with me. After all, I hardly think she's Adam Simmond's girl friend."

"She's Jean Clayton," he said. "We're engaged."

"Well, well!" There was a mischievous look on her face. "And what does your grandfather think of that?"

When he remained silent she went on:

"He was head over heels with delight when Mark told him he was going to marry me. It was the answer to his prayer. With me as Mark's wife my father would let his land go, or so the Laird thought. Then Mark dirtied his ticket—and that was the end of another man's dream!"

There was bitterness in the young voice now. He glanced at her. Her limp was more pronounced now. He said:

"You ought to be in the saddle. You're not really fit to walk all the way to the farm."

She shook her head.

"I'm all right!" she exclaimed defensively.

"Let me help you up."

He was standing very close to her. He could see the rise and fall of her breasts under the thin shirt she wore beneath her unbuttoned jacket. There was something vital about this girl. Perhaps it was something to do with the fresh, salty air, or perhaps it was her Celtic blood.

He put his arms about her and swung her up into the saddle. She smiled down at him.

"You're a very masterful young man, Andrew Murray," she said.

He said nothing to this, not sure if it was intended to be a compliment or not, but reached for the trailing reins and led the horse along the road.

They turned a corner and there, over-looking the sea, was the Campbell farm-stead, nestling low against the slope of the ground. An open gate admitted them to a track which led across a field to the house.

"You'd better come in and meet father now you're here," Fiona said.

Andrew reached up to lift her from the saddle. Just for a moment he held her close. Her warm breath was on his cheek. He felt a sudden excitement.

"Please!" she said and he released her quickly.

She limped ahead of him to the house. He noticed a big car stood in the stack-yard, a man seated at the wheel. As they went by he raised his hand in salute to Fiona and gave Andrew a curious look.

"I think my father has visitors," Fiona said. "That's the local taxi."

"I won't come in then," Andrew said, but she shook her head.

"Of course you must. Daddy will be very cross if I tell him you were here but went away without coming in to have a word with him."

"But his visitors?"

"They're not important. They'll be oil men. They've been here before."

She led the way into the house. He followed wondering what oil men were doing on Bleiside Island. Did they think there was oil on Mr. Campbell's land?

He heard voices as they crossed a big kitchen and came out into a square hall. A door on the left was half open. Fiona made for it.

Three men were seated by the fire. They looked round as the two young people came into the room. The oldest —a grey-haired man with arthritic hands resting on a stick—smiled as his daughter went to his side and kissed his lined cheek.

"Daddy, this is Andrew Murray," she said and before he could speak: "He caught Prince after I'd been thrown."

"You're not hurt?" There was anxiety in the deep voice.

"I turned my knee but it's nothing serious."

Mr. Campbell studied Andrew carefully.

"So you're Angus Murray's long-lost grandson, eh?" he said.

Andrew nodded. "Yes. I arrived on the island this morning."

"So I heard." Mr. Campbell looked at the two men in well-cut business suits who had risen from their chairs and were standing rather awkwardly looking at the newcomers. "This is Mr. Marchant and this Mr. Blake. They're here on business."

Andrew smiled and the two men gave him a rather bleak look and a nod. He had been about to extend his hand, but thought better of it.

"I won't stay, Mr. Campbell," he said, "I can see you're busy. But it's nice to have met you."

"Give the Laird my best wishes," the other said and there was a hint of sarcasm in his voice.

Fiona followed him from the room.

"I'm sorry I let you in for that," she said. "But I wanted Daddy to meet you."

A pleasant-faced young woman was coming down the staircase into the hall. Fiona looked at Andrew.

"This is Jessie Mackenzie," she said. "She helps me about the house. This is Mr. Murray, Jessie."

The woman gave Andrew a broad smile.

"Welcome to Bleiside Island, sir," she said. "Paddy Toller who brought the gentlemen from the boat said he'd seen you arrive this morning."

He caught Fiona's glance and saw the twinkle in her eyes. Everybody knows everybody's business, they seemed to say. He smiled at the servant and turned away.

"I'd better be getting back to the castle," he said.

She accompanied him to the kitchen door.

"Thank you for helping me," she said. "I hope your knee will soon be well again."

"I'm sure it will."

Giving him a last smile she turned and hurried back into the house again. Andrew stood for a moment outside the door. The taxi-driver was watching him. He began to walk slowly back down the rutted track to the gate.

So Fiona Campbell had been about to marry his cousin Mark. And Angus Murray had been "Head over heels with delight." But now the marriage might not take place. The more Andrew learnt about the situation on Bleiside Island, the more complicated it became. And now there were oil-men at the Campbell farm!

9

JEAN crouched at the foot of the cliff. She was exhausted. She had shouted till she was hoarse. She had even tried to climb the steep cliff to the castle high above but had been defeated by an overhang that would let her go no further. She could see ledges on which the gulls were nesting higher up the cliff, but there was no way of reaching them.

The spring evening was closing in. She had been in the little cove for about an hour, though it seemed far longer.

Now the tide had advanced almost to her feet. Only about eighteen inches of sand were left between the advancing waves and the foot of the cliff.

She looked towards the rocks over which she had scrambled an hour before.

They had vanished completely under the rising tide. Now the waves were flinging themselves at the cliff in a frenzy of snow-white water.

She fought down the panic that threatened to sweep over her. The tide was still rising. Soon she would be driven to climb as far as she could up the cliff.

There she would have to cling until the tide turned. That might be hours ahead. And then it would be dark.

And she had no way of telling how high the waves reached. She looked again at one possible place of shelter on the cliff. It would not take much to sweep her from such a precarious perch.

In this strong tide she might be swept far out to sea and never be seen again.

Her disappearance would be a complete mystery to Peter—and everybody else at the castle.

Would they start a search for her believing she had gone for a walk and lost herself on the trackless moors which made up three-quarters of the island?

But they would not find her until— until her body was washed ashore either on Bleiside or one of the other islands in the sound.

She looked despairingly out to sea.

If only she was a strong swimmer she might have risked the currents and tried to swim round the rocks at the foot of the cliff and gained the sands at the other side.

But she knew she would not succeed. Her swimming had been confined to the occasional visit to an indoor swimming pool, and to seaside holidays on coasts where the currents were much less powerful. If she attempted to swim out of the cove she would certainly be dashed against the rocks by the turbulent waves.

Something moved on the water. The setting sun had turned the sea into a shimmering golden lake. The dazzle was such as to make it almost impossible to identify the object that caught her eye.

Then, shading her eyes with her hand, she realised that the dark object on the water was a small boat. Above the thunder of the waves she believed she could hear the put-put of an outboard motor.

She stood up, pulled her coat off and started waving it wildly above her head.

She shouted, too, but had little hope that anyone in the boat would hear her above the noise of the waves.

The boat went on its way. She could now see the figure of a man at the helm. He did not show any sign that he had seen her.

Despair filled her. She jumped up and down, waving the coat and yelling at the top of her voice.

Then suddenly she saw the boat change direction.

A few seconds later she was certain, and hope surged through her.

The boatman had seen her. He was heading the craft towards the shore, where already one wave, more vigorous than its fellows, had covered her feet.

Now she could see the figure in the boat more clearly. He was a big, middle-aged man wearing a blue jersey. A peaked cap covering his head shaded his face. But she could make out a heavy, reddish moustache and beard which almost obscured his mouth and chin.

He beached the little boat within a few yards of her.

"Run for it, miss!" he yelled. "I can't hold it here for more than a minute or so."

She obeyed with alacrity. A moment later she was scrambling aboard. The little engine and the boat almost swamped by an incoming wave, regained the comparatively calm water a few yards out from the cliff.

"And what were you doing there with the tide coming in?" Jean's rescuer demanded; then staring at her: "But of course you're a stranger. Arrived on the island this very morning, eh?"

"Yes? How did you know?" she asked.

She was shivering. She pulled her coat over her shoulders and tried desperately to stop her teeth from chattering.

"Here, have a drop of this!" he said, producing a small flask from his hip pocket. "You look frozen to the very bone."

She took the cap off the flask and sipped the whisky. It made her gasp. She felt as if a fire was coursing through her.

"Thank you!" she handed the flask back. He took a swig and put the whisky in his hip pocket again.

"Feel a little better?" he grinned.

"Yes, thank you."

"So you've come to stay with the Laird, eh?" he asked.

She nodded. "You haven't told me how you know. Did you see the steamer come into the harbour this morning?"

"I did that! I said to meself: 'This is the Laird's grandson and that must be his young leddy. Come all the way from England!'"

"But how could you possibly know— about me, I mean?"

He tapped his nose with a thick forefinger and winked.

"There are few secrets here on Bleiside. You'll sure enough find that out for yourself—if you stay long enough."

110

She frowned. What did he mean—if she stayed long enough?

He laughed. He had plainly guessed her thoughts.

"My name's Tam McTavish," he said. "I make a living lobstering. In summer I take people out fishing in my boat."

He nodded at the box beside him. She saw the sinister black lobsters twisting and turning in it. He had obviously been emptying his lobster pots just before he had rescued her.

"And what did the Laird say when you arrived at the castle?" the fisherman asked and there was a sly twinkle in his eyes. "Didn't give you too good a welcome, I'll be bound!"

Jean frowned. How could he know?

"Why do you say that?"

"Because he wasn't expecting ye, that's what. He thought his grandson would be all alone and fancy free."

The little boat was moving erratically through the choppy sea, seeming to climb over each wave then dive into the trough beyond.

111

What with the swell and the draught of whisky, which she wasn't used to, Jean felt queasy. She hoped she wasn't going to be sick. The little fishing boat was very different from the squat steady bulk of the steamer which had crossed to the island that morning. It seemed to make no attempt to cut through the waves but bobbed up and over them like a cork.

"He's a funny old gentleman is the Laird," Tam McTavish said. "A funny old gentleman, indeed. I dare say you'll find that out for yourself if you stay long on the island."

She felt slightly annoyed. Why was this stranger talking to her like this? She said brusquely:

"I don't think we should discuss Mr. Murray in this way."

He made no reply, and Jean at once felt a little ashamed of herself. After all, if he hadn't come along when he did she might have been drowned.

"I'm sorry," she said. "I shouldn't have spoken like that."

He smiled reassuringly. "I suppose I

was trying to warn ye. I know the Laird, you see. He's not a man to let anyone upset his plans."

"What plans?" she asked, puzzled.

"They're plans that don't include you, missy," he said shortly. "Anything that gets between the Laird and owning the Campbell land will get short shrift!"

"And how do you think I should do that?"

"You will if you marry that young man of yours, the Laird's grandson. The old gentleman has other plans for your sweetheart, missy."

"What plans?"

"Mr. Campbell has a very pretty daughter. She would have married Mr. Mark if—well, if Mr. Mark hadn't made a fool of himself and got himself sent to prison."

Jean's heart sank. She knew what this man meant. If Fiona Campbell didn't marry Mark she might be inclined to settle for another Murray—Andrew.

She longed to cry out: "But Peter would never do that. He loves me. He's

113

told his grandfather so. If the Laird insists on him marrying another girl he'll tell him to leave the estate to someone else."

But she kept silent. She was not going to discuss her—and Peter's affairs—with this fisherman.

The harbour wall drew nearer. Soon they had left the uneasy sea outside and were moving across the calm water to a flight of stone steps which ran up to the quay.

Jean smiled at McTavish.

"Thank you for saving my life," she said sincerely. "I might have drowned if you hadn't seen me at the foot of the cliff."

"I was glad to be of service, miss," he said, touching his cap.

As she stood up and made to step from the boat on to the step, he said:

"Mind what I've just been saying to ye, missy. The Laird is a difficult man. What he says goes on Bleiside Island. Get that young man of yours to take you away, that's my advice. There's only unhappiness for you at Arachnock Castle!"

She stood on the step and looked back at him. She wanted to say something to him, something that would shake his conviction that there was nothing but trouble for her here, but before she could form any words, he had let in the clutch and the little boat headed off across the harbour towards its mooring at the far side.

While she watched, Tam McTavish did not give her another glance.

She climbed the stone steps to the quay. How was she going to get back to the castle? It was at least three miles from the village of Bleiside.

A car was standing a little further along the quay. A man climbed from the driver's seat and walked towards her. He was dressed in a rather shabby blue uniform and wore a peaked cap.

Jean did not know it but this was Toller, the local taxi driver, who had returned only a short while before with the two oil men he had earlier driven out to the Campbell farm.

His passengers were now in the local inn waiting for the steamer to call at Bleiside on its return trip from the islands.

"Can I offer my services, miss?" he asked.

Toller had a long sallow face and small, sharp eyes. His accent was not that of the Western Isles.

"Are you a taxi driver?" Jean asked.

"I am, indeed, miss. That's my taxi further along the quay."

"I want to go to Arachnock Castle," she said.

"Very well, miss. This way, please."

He led the way to the car and opened the rear door. Jean was soon seated in the back of the old Austin.

As they drove out of the village and took the road to Arachnock Toller looked over his shoulder at Jean.

"And how do you like our island, miss? Though perhaps you've not been here long enough to judge."

"It's very beautiful," she replied.

Here was someone else who knew all that was going on, she thought. No doubt he, too, had seen her arrive with Peter at the island earlier that day. She wondered if he too was about to offer her advice.

Presently they were passing the Campbell farm. The driver nodded towards the white-washed buildings which appeared to be crouching to escape the fierce wind off the sea. Unlike the castle, Jean thought, which boldly confronted the weather, impregnable to storm or gale.

"I saw the young gentleman when I was at the farm earlier," he said.

"The young gentleman!" she exclaimed.

"The Laird's grandson. He caught Miss Fiona Campbell's horse when it threw her—a brave act. He brought her back to the farm. He met her father."

So Peter had met Fiona Campbell soon after they had parted and she had gone on her ill-fated walk along the shore!

"How do you know all this?" she

asked, genuinely interested. What curious people these were. They seemed able to pluck their knowledge out of the air.

"Jessie Mackenzie, the Campbell's house body, told me after Mr. Andrew had gone. I was waiting for my passengers to take them back to catch the steamer to the mainland."

After a moment or two he said:

"You'll be the lassie who's to marry Mr. Andrew, eh?"

The sallow face turned to glance back at her in the back of the old taxi. She bit her lip. She had no intention of gossiping about Peter with this man.

He saw by her expression that his question had not pleased her. He turned back to stare through the windscreen again.

"The Laird's a good man if a strange one," he said as if to himself. Jean steeled herself for more mysterious warnings about Angus Murray's character. But Toller said no more until the taxi was entering the castle courtyard.

When she had paid him off—luckily

118

she had her purse in her pocket—Jean went into the castle.

The big entrance hall was empty, but as she turned to the stairs the library door opened and Andrew looked out.

"Jean, where have you been?" he cried, making towards her.

She did not feel like producing a long explanation. And, at the moment, she did not want to talk to Peter.

"For a walk along the shore," she said. "I'm just going up to my room. I shall have a bath and perhaps lie down for a while. I'm very tired." With an uncertain smile, she moved away.

He watched her in silence as she crossed to the stairs. When she had disappeared he turned back to the library. The door was still open and Adam appeared.

"Was that your fiancée?" he asked.

"Yes. She says she's been for a walk along the shore. Must have been a very long walk."

"But the tide's up. She might have been cut off," Adam exclaimed.

"She probably was," Andrew declared drily. "She certainly didn't look like someone who's just been for a pleasant saunter!"

He passed Adam, who barely succeeded in concealing his surprise at Peter's callous reaction, and made for the fire at the far side of the big room.

Why was Jean acting so strangely? he wondered. First of all she had been so unreasonable about his conversation with his grandfather. Now she had treated him quite coldly, walking off without saying why she had been out so long. And there had been a look in her eyes, when she spoke to him in the hall, that gave him an uneasy feeling.

"Perhaps she'll tell me more when she's not quite so tired," he decided and held out his hands to the blaze in the big fireplace.

10

JEAN had a hot bath in the bathroom near her room. One surprising thing about the rather draughty castle, she decided, was that there was always an inexhaustible supply of piping hot water.

She went back to her room. The hot water had dissolved much of the tiredness from her aching, chilled body. She lay on the bed and covered herself with a thick, slightly musty eiderdown, whose original pattern of flowers had faded so much it was hard to distinguish.

She would lie down for half an hour or so, she decided, then she would go downstairs. It was getting late, and soon it would be time for dinner.

But she felt so warm and relaxed that she quickly fell asleep.

She wakened with a start. The room was almost dark. Someone was knocking on the door.

She slipped off the bed and, pulling a thin wrap over her shoulders, went to the door. She opened it to find Mrs. Baird in the corridor outside.

"Dinner's ready, miss," she said eyeing Jean curiously. "The Laird does not like waiting for his meal," she added apologetically. "Perhaps you could come down as soon as possible."

"I'm sorry. I must have fallen asleep," Jean said.

"You're feeling all right, I hope, miss?" The woman's good-natured face was anxious.

"Yes, I'm fine!" Jean smiled. "I'll be down shortly."

She closed the door and went to put on the only dress she had brought with her, a plain brown skirt and white top which she had bought in the sales. It matched her soft brown eyes and hair. Peter had admired it more than once.

She glanced in the mirror before leaving the room. She thought again of that girl she had seen on the grey horse that morning as she rode in the Rolls to the castle, the girl Peter had evidently spent some time with when she was walking into danger on the shore.

What was the girl like? she wondered. Had Peter liked her? Did he know that she had been due to marry his cousin Mark thereby ensuring that the Campbell land would pass into the possession of the Murrays?

She went downstairs. Mrs. Baird was crossing the hall to the dining room, bearing a tray of china.

"The others are in the sitting room, miss," she said, and nodded towards a door at the far side of the hall.

Jean crossed to it and opened it. It was a large room crowded with old-fashioned furniture. The Laird was standing with his back to the blazing log fire in the stone fireplace. The others were grouped about him. They were all holding glasses.

As Jean entered they turned to look at her. The Laird made a great business of consulting his watch.

"Ah, here she is!" he declared, then as if remembering he was the host: "Would you care for a glass of sherry, Miss Clayton?"

"I'm sorry to be late," she replied. "I was very tired—it must be all the sea air —and I fell asleep."

"My grandfather asked you if you'd like a glass of sherry!" Andrew said rather sharply.

"No, thank you," Jean said, a little taken aback by his tone.

She met Mrs. Anderson's eyes. They were unfriendly. There was a supercilious smile on the thin lips. She's glad I've kept the Laird waiting, she thought.

"Then we can go in to dinner," the old man said.

He put his glass down, looked at his daughter, then led the way to the door. Adam and his grandson followed, Jean walking between them.

The meal was simple but beautifully cooked. There was a vegetable broth followed by hot lobster in a cream sauce. Jean thought of Tam McTavish. Had he supplied the lobster?

Adam made a brave attempt to keep

the conversation going. He sensed the tenseness between the Laird and his grandson, and felt sorry for Jean who must have realised by now how unwelcome she was at Arachnock Castle.

"You went for a walk on the shore?" he questioned. "You must have just escaped being cut off by the tide."

She shook her head.

"I was cut off," she said quietly, and went on to tell how Tam McTavish had rescued her when the first wave had reached the foot of the cliffs and threatened to sweep her out to sea.

"It was a foolish thing to do," Andrew said. "Surely you must have seen that the tide was rising."

"She could hardly be expected to have a tide table with her," Adam declared with a smile. "I suppose Tam took you back to the harbour?"

"Yes. I then came alone to the castle in a taxi."

"You were lucky!" the Laird growled. "I gather Toller's been pretty busy today."

Andrew, sitting next to his grandfather, gave the Laird a sharp glance. So he knows about the oil men who visited Mr. Campbell today, he thought. Another instance of the Bleiside grapevine at work.

"Oh, is Toller the taxi driver?" said Jean. "He told me he'd taken two men from the Campbell Farm to Bleiside to wait for the steamer back to the mainland."

She noticed that Mrs. Anderson's eyes were on her father. They were worried eyes, as if their owner knew what was passing through the old man's mind.

At last the meal was over, much to Jean's relief. The Laird said he would take his coffee in his study and invited Adam to accompany him.

Mrs. Anderson disappeared, evidently to her own quarters. Jean and Andrew went to the library where they found their coffee waiting for them before the fire.

"And now tell me what really happened this afternoon," Andrew said, taking his cup from Jean.

"When you went striding off I decided

126

to take a walk along the shore," she said. "That's all that really happened, as you put it!"

"But this isn't Eastbourne, you know. You must have seen it was dangerous."

"It didn't occur to me. In any case, I was feeling a bit unhappy at the way you walked off like that. I wasn't thinking about the tide."

"I was angry! I didn't think you really appreciated my position here at the castle."

"You mean, as your grandfather's heir?"

He nodded. He was scowling at the fire.

"Have you made up your mind yet?" she asked and waited anxiously for his reply.

He shrugged. "It's early days to make such an important decision. I'm not convinced it's a matter of either/or. My grandfather's not a completely unreasonable man. He may see things my way."

"But if Adam Simmonds has come to Bleiside to make a new will for your grandfather, he'll want to know whether it's to be yes or no pretty quickly," she exclaimed. "He'll want to get back to London—he must have other clients who need attention. He can't stay indefinitely until you make your mind up."

He stared at her directly.

"And what do you think I ought to do?" he demanded. "My decision affects you as much as it affects me."

"You know your grandfather dislikes me. He makes no bones about that. What sort of life would we have here at the castle with him feeling as he does about me?"

"He's an old man," he muttered. "He won't live forever."

She looked at him sharply. Surely that was a callous thing to say!

She changed the subject abruptly.

"I hear you met Fiona Campbell and went back to her father's farm to meet Mr. Campbell," she said.

"Yes. Her horse threw her. She was hurt so I went back to the farm with her."

"Did you like her?"

"Yes, and I liked her father. I can't see why my grandfather objects to him so violently."

"Do you know what they're saying on Bleiside?" she asked and when he did not speak: "They're saying that now Mark, your cousin, has gone to prison, your grandfather will expect *you* to marry Fiona Campbell."

She saw the colour rise in his cheeks. His eyes flashed.

"Of all the nonsense I ever heard!" he cried.

"It's not nonsense at all. No wonder he was shaken when you turned up at the castle with me."

"I'm marrying you and the sooner he realises that the better!" he said violently.

There was something in his voice, a certain bluster, that told her he was not entirely sincere in what he said.

Had he been attracted to Fiona Campbell?

She was a very pretty girl, and if she had given her former lover up now he was

129

in prison then she might look upon Peter
—Andrew—as a good substitute.

She thought longingly of their home
town, of the future that had seemed only
a couple of days ago to be opening out so
happily for them both. Now—now a dark
cloud had come into her sky to cast a
shadow over her hopes.

Tears welled into her eyes. She turned
her head away so that the man by her side
should not see them.

She felt Andrew's hand cover hers.

"Let's leave the whole thing for
tonight," he begged. "We're both tired.
Everything will seem very different in the
morning."

"Will you have decided what to do?"
she asked.

"I think so," he said and with that she
had to be content.

She put her cup down. She stood up
and looked down at him. The momentary
weakness had been overcome, and she
had regained her composure. When she
spoke, her voice was firm.

"If you still tell me you haven't made

up your mind when I see you in the morning, I shall go back to the mainland," she said.

Without waiting for him to reply, she turned quickly away and made for the door.

In his study the Laird looked across his desk at the handsome young English solicitor seated opposite. He would rather have done business with his father, but this young fellow seemed sharp enough.

"You realise what it will mean if these people who called on Campbell today really do think they can find oil on his land?" he demanded.

"If they do—and it's a big if—it will mean life will be a lot easier for him, I imagine," Adam murmured.

The Laird jumped up with an agility suprising for a man of his age, and began to pace up and down the room.

"Campell's on the verge of bankruptcy," he cried. "I know that for a fact. If all had gone as it should have done I'd have had that Campbell land as my own

131

within the year. It wouldn't have mattered whether my grandson Mark had married Fiona Campbell or not. Her father would have been forced to sell. Now, though, things have changed. If there's oil on that land Campbell could be a rich man!"

Adam shook his head.

"I think that assumption is premature," he said. "The mere fact that some alleged representatives from an oil company have been to discuss certain matters—we don't know exactly what—with Mr. Campbell doesn't mean to say Campbell's suddenly going to become rich. There's a great deal to be done before the existence of oil can be confirmed. We can probably assume that a favourable geological survey had been made. The next step would be test drillings. That could take a year or two at least. And in the end the whole thing might turn out to be a flop."

"But don't you see, man!" the other cried irritably, "if these men believe oil is there—and they must, as you say, have some evidence for their belief—they'll make sure no one else gets hold of the land by offering Campbell a pretty big sum just to guard their interests. That will put Campbell on Easy Street whether there's oil there or not. He doesn't want to sell to me, even if I could match the figure an oil company is likely to offer. I'm an old man, Simmonds. I've waited a long time for that land. I'm damned if I'll let it be snatched away now."

"There's little you can do. Why don't you forget Campbell and his land, sir? You own ninety per cent of Bleiside Island as it is. I don't understand why a few more acres should matter one way or the other."

The Laird glared at him across the desk—a look of pure rage. He raised a clenched fist, almost as if he would strike the younger man.

"How the devil can you say that, Simmonds?" he cried hoarsely. "Your father knew my dreams. You should know it too. It's simple enough. I mean to own all of Bleiside Island before I die.

That's what I intend to pass on to my heir, the man who follows me. My grandson, Andrew!"

"But if Mr Campbell's financial position improves sufficiently so that he is not forced to sell . . ."

The old man's eyes narrowed. He leant forward, lowering his voice conspiratorially.

"Listen to me, Simmonds. There is another way whereby the Campbell land could become part of the Murray estate. You know the recent history of my family. I think you can guess what way I mean?"

Adam's mouth tightened. He knew very well what was in his client's mind.

"I suppose you think that if Andrew and Fiona Campbell. . . ?"

"Exactly! If Andrew marries Fiona, the Campbell land will be added automatically to the Murray property when her father dies."

"But, sir, as I've pointed out before, Andrew's already engaged to another girl. You can't expect him simply to give up the girl he is about to marry" (Adam had been about to say "the girl he loves") "purely for your own convenience, and to add a few relatively insignificant acres to the estate."

"The girl he loves!" the old man snorted. "Believe me, Simmonds, I'm a judge of character. That grandson of mine may think he loves his little typist, but I think he will change his mind when he understands where his true interests lie! No," he held up a hand to stop Adam interrupting, "I believe the thought of being Laird of Arachnock—When he thinks it over—will appeal to him much more than being a damned shop assistant scraping up the mortgage payments for a three-bedroomed semi every month and married to a dull little typist, pretty or not!"

He opened a drawer in his desk and picked up a sheet of paper. After glancing briefly at it, he handed it over to the young solicitor. Adam took it with some reluctance.

"I've set down my wishes in respect to

my new will," said Angus Murray. "You'd better get back to London tomorrow, Simmonds, and draw up a proper document, which I'll sign when you return."

Adam glanced at the paper.

"I see you've made Andrew your heir —in spite of everything," he said.

The other nodded.

"By the time you've drawn up the will and brought it back for me to sign I think matters will have taken a turn for the better."

"By that you mean?"

The Laird stroked his beard. There was a look in the deep-set eyes which chilled Adam's heart.

"I mean exactly what I say," the deep voice said. "By the time you return matters will have taken a turn for the better. And now, that will be all for tonight. I'm an old man. Will you take a dram with me before bed?"

He took a heavy crystal decanter from a cupboard in the corner of the study, waited until Adam shook his head, and returned to his chair carrying a single tumbler.

Adam opened his mouth to say something more, thought better of it and, after a gruff "Good night" left the room.

What was the old devil up to? he wondered as he made his way slowly towards the library. He had an unhappy feeling that it would not benefit Andrew's fiancée in any way.

The thought troubled him deeply. Ever since they had bumped into each other in the corridor of the train, he had been aware of feeling protective towards her. Protective? No, more than that . . .

It was Jean who had made him stop to consider his bachelor life, and wonder whether there wasn't something better for him in the future. She did seem the sort of girl who would make a marvellous wife. But of course he had not thought of her in that role for himself. She was engaged to Andrew.

But would she ever marry Andrew? Not if the Laird of Arachnock Castle had his way.

What did the old man mean by "matters taking a turn for the better"? There was no way he could stop Andrew marrying Jean—if that was what Andrew was determined to do.

But was Andrew determined? Angus Murray thought he had detected a weakness in the young man, a sign that he would prefer Arachnock Castle and all that went with it to the love of Jean Clayton.

Adam had to admit, to himself at least, that Angus Murray might be correct. Andrew had struck him as a pleasant enough young man. But there was a selfish, ambitious streak in him—not surprising, as he was a Murray.

Yes, Jean was the person he felt sorry for. It was so unfair, a sweet girl like that . . . .

When he arrived at the door of the library, his handsome face was grimly set.

11

JEAN slept little that night. Dawn was showing round the edges of the heavy curtains and she was still tossing and turning.

At last, knowing she would not sleep any more, she threw back the covers and got out of bed.

She went to the window and drew back the curtains. It was now broad daylight, and the rays of the sun glinted on the dark sea. With the sleeping islands on the horizon the scene was breathtakingly beautiful.

"I'll go for a walk," Jean thought, "but not on the beach!" Dressing quickly, she stole from her room, along the silent corridor and tip-toed down the stairs.

She could hear the faint murmur of voices from somewhere deep in the inner recesses of the old building. Evidently someone was already working in the kitchen though it was still early, barely six o'clock.

She slid back a bolt and let herself out into the courtyard. Soon she reached the road, and headed towards Bleiside. After a half a mile or so, she spotted a track which led up on to the moor and took it.

Soon she was making her way through a vast sea of purple heather. Seagulls screamed overhead, soaring in the wind against a brilliant sky. Occasionally there was a rustle near at hand as some small creatures, disturbed by her footfall, moved hurriedly away.

She felt released from the tensions of the night out here in the solitude of the moor. As she had lain sleepless during the night she had not been able to see things clearly.

No solution to her present predicament had presented itself, as she tossed and turned endlessly in the big old bed.

Out here, in the crisp morning air, things seemed simple and clear-cut. The wind brought a sparkle to her eyes and swept the confusion from her mind.

"If Peter still can't make his mind up this morning, I'll do exactly what I said I'd do;" she thought. "I'll take the steamer to the mainland and catch the first train to Glasgow, then home. If he stills wants me he can come after me. If he doesn't he must stay here on Bleiside Island and make a new life for himself as his grandfather's heir."

After she had been walking for half an hour she decided she had better turn back. A glance at her watch told her it was past seven o'clock. She would not reach the castle until at least eight o'clock.

She had been late for dinner on the previous night. It would not do to be late for breakfast this morning!

As she made along the path towards the road she noticed another path on her left striking off across the heather to higher ground.

She calculated that if she took it she ought to reach the road much nearer the castle than if she kept straight on the way she was going.

She did not hesitate but struck out at

once up the slope. She climbed steadily for ten minutes or so and soon reached a point where she found herself looking down on the sea with the road a quarter of a mile below her.

Two people were standing in the middle of the road. A horse was cropping the short grass under the wall which lined the narrow road.

Jean's heart gave a little jump. There was no mistaking who the two young people were on the road below.

Fiona Campbell—and Peter!

They were talking animatedly together. Fiona was smiling up into the young man's face and he was laughing at something she had evidently said. She had not seen him laugh like that since they arrived on Bleiside Island.

Jean hesitated. If she retreated from the higher ground she could find her way back to the castle out of sight of the couple below.

Then she asked herself why she should be furtive. If Peter had arranged an early-morning meeting with Fiona Campbell when he had seen her on the previous day it might be as well if he knew she had seen him.

She started down the slope. They did not see her coming at first, but as she approached the wall the girl looked round. She said something to her companion who also looked round.

"Hello, Jean!" he called as she reached the low wall and stepped over it. "I came out for an early morning walk. I met Miss Campbell who tells me she often rides this way before breakfast."

Fiona smiled at Jean.

"Good morning," she said. "Isn't it a lovely day?"

"Yes. I wakened early and like Peter— I mean Andrew—I decided to have a walk. I just couldn't stay in bed with the sun shining."

"We'd better get back to the castle," Andrew said. "Breakfast is at eight-thirty. I asked Mrs. Baird."

Fiona picked up the horse's reins. As she started to mount Jean asked:

"How are you today, Miss Campbell?

143

Andrew told me your horse threw you yesterday."

"Oh, I'm all right," the other girl smiled. "A bit stiff. It was just a bruise. Your fiancé kindly saw me home."

She smiled at Andrew, nodded at Jean then turned the horse and trotted off along the road back towards her father's farm.

"She's a very pretty girl," Jean exclaimed.

"Think so?" he said, as if the thought had not occurred to him until she mentioned it.

As they approached the castle she drew a deep breath. There might not be a better opportunity to talk to him than now.

"Have you decided anything?" she asked, looking up at him as they walked along side by side.

He frowned. "Oh, can't we leave it until after breakfast?"

She shook her head. Her eyes flashed.

"Why do you always put me off?" she asked. "Surely you must know whether you want to stay at the castle as your grandfather's heir—or return home."

He looked round, at the shining sea on one hand and the purple moor on the other.

"I don't think I want to go back home," he said in a low voice. "I'm beginning to like it here."

"Well, that's something," she said. "Now, all you've to decide about is—me."

"About you?" He frowned. "What do you mean?"

"Are you going to tell your grandfather you'd like to become his heir—with me as your wife?"

"Well, of course, with you as my wife!"

"I don't believe he'll agree. You've seen for yourself he doesn't like me. He wants you to marry Fiona Campbell—to take Mark's place there as well."

"But he hates the Campbells!"

She shook her head sadly.

"Oh, my dear, he doesn't want you to marry Fiona because he *likes* her. He wants you to marry her so that he can add

145

her father's farm and its land to his own. He wants to be king of Bleiside Island, and he can't be that until he owns every acre."

"You're talking nonsense!" he said crossly.

"I'm not! If there's a chance of oil being found on Mr. Campbell's land, and Mr. Campbell snaps his fingers in your grandfather's face, your marrying Fiona is the last card he has to play. If she became your wife the Campbell farm and all that goes with it—oil, the lot—would come to the Laird of Arachnock whoever he might be: you or your grandfather."

"You always did have a vivid imagination," Andrew cried, laughing the whole thing off as preposterous.

"Well, think it over, Peter. I'll willingly go with you if you want to talk to your grandfather about our getting married. If you don't want to take the bull by the horns and go on hesitating I shall go back to the mainland today—by myself."

"You're being childish now!" he said

angrily, and before she could speak again: "And I wish you'd stop calling me 'Peter'. It isn't my name and you know it!"

She walked ahead of him up the slope to the castle. In the courtyard, before they went into the gaunt building she turned and faced him.

"I mean what I've just said," she said. "Either you tell your grandfather that you mean to marry me whether he makes you his heir or not. If you don't agree to do that I shall go back home by myself. I'll know then that you don't want to marry me!"

He said nothing to this but stared after her with a frown on his good-looking face as she mounted the steps and disappeared into the castle.

12

FIONA CAMPBELL found herself thinking of Andrew Murray as she cantered along the road back to her father's farm.

He was very different from his cousin, Mark. Not as aggressive, not as arrogant, not as demanding. Mark had been heir to Arachnock and he never let people forget it.

All the islanders liked him for that, just as they liked the Laird, who Mark very much resembled. Mark's father had been the same type. They were an arrogant lot, those Murrays.

But although they were hard, tough men who usually got their own way, with the Murray toughness there went a strange, wayward charm.

It was this charm that had bowled her over, Fiona thought with a wry smile. Mark had certainly had his share of it, even when they were children together.

It must have been the same Murray charm that had captivated Andrew's mother all those years ago, before Fiona was born, when James Murray had brought her to Bleiside Island. Her father had told her the story—how Andrew had been born at the castle, from which his mother had fled with her baby after her husband had died at the wheel of his car.

Fiona remembered the terrible shock she had suffered when the man she loved had been arrested and sent to prison.

At first she had wandered round in a mist of despair. That Mark could get mixed up in something as dreadful as dealing in drugs . . . It was too horrible to think about.

Her father, as horrified as she was, had forbidden her to write to Mark in prison.

"You've finished with him, my dear," he had told her. "I was against you getting mixed up with those Murrays in the first place. This is the last straw. I'm told even his grandfather has disowned him. Well, you'll disown him as well."

She wondered what her father had thought of Andrew when she had taken him back to the farm on the previous day. He had seemed to like him. Certainly he had not forbidden her to see him again even though he was as much a Murray as Mark was.

But her father was a sick man. The old fight had gone out of him. Things had not gone right on the farm for a long time. Debts had piled up. The fear of bankruptcy was ever present. Her father seldom talked about it. But the signs were obvious.

Then those oil men had come on the scene and new hope had been born. Her father, though still frail, had brightened up since their visit. It might be a long time before it was certain that oil did lie under Campbell land, but the oil company was prepared to pay a substantial sum to find out.

If no oil was found her father would

not be the loser, Fiona thought, and that was the important thing.

She stabled her horse and went into the house. Jessie Mackenzie called from the stove where she was cooking bacon and eggs:

"Breakfast's nearly ready, my dear. Your father's staying in bed. He's not feeling so well this morning."

There was nothing unusual about this and Fiona, after she had washed her hands at the sink, sat at the table, where Jessie placed a well-filled plate before her and a steaming teapot to hand.

She ate with a rare appetite. There was nothing like a brisk ride before breakfast, she thought, as she cut into the delicious home-cured bacon.

Later, she took up a cup of tea to her father's room. He smiled wanly from his pillow.

"How do you feel, Daddy?" Fiona asked, putting the cup on the bedside table.

"Very tired," he replied. "Discussing

business with those two oil men yesterday took it out of me."

"You'd better stay in bed all day."

"But the farm, Fiona! I can't just lie here when there's so much to do. With Jock away too, it would be difficult to get everything done even if I were fully fit."

"Jessie and I can manage! It won't be the first time and you've never had cause to complain, have you?"

A faint smile lit the pale face.

"You're a good lass, Fiona," he said. "I'll see how I feel by mid-day."

She went downstairs. When the indoor chores were done she and Jessie Mackenzie divided the outside work between them. Jock Blezard, the handyman, had flu and would be away for several days yet, the doctor had said.

There were cows to be milked, chickens to be fed, feed to be ordered by telephone for dispatch by steamer from the mainland—a score of other jobs to be attended to.

About the middle of the morning Fiona stretched her aching back, gave the cow she had just milked a friendly pat and turned with her full bucket of creamy milk to empty it into the waiting container. Later, it would be picked up by lorry to be taken to Bleiside and loaded on the steamer to the mainland.

A man was leaning against the side of the doorway leading into the byre. The sun was behind him and she could only make out a silhouette. Fiona frowned. Who was this? Some travelling salesman come to try and get an order for cattle feed? As this was the only farm on the island, apart from Angus Murray's tenants, few salesmen bothered to make the trip.

She put the bucket down and went towards him. With his back to the light she could not see his face.

But there was something about the set of his shoulders that she recognised. Her heart quickened. She knew who he was before he spoke.

"Hello, Fiona. Didn't expect to see me, eh!"

"Mark!"

153

"Yes, your sweetheart, Mark, fresh from Her Majesty's custody!" he said, and there was a note of bitterness in his voice. When she did not move, he asked ironically, "Aren't you going to give me a kiss?"

"But, Mark, how did you. . . ? I mean, I thought you were not. . . ?"

He laughed, a harsh sound with no humour in it.

"Oh, I didn't escape, if that's what you're thinking," he said. "I'm not on the run. Believe it or not they found they had miscalculated my remission for good conduct. Forgotten to allow for time spent in gaol before the trial, or something of the sort. I never quite understood." He gave a mirthless grin. "I suspect they just wanted to get rid of me —bad effect on the other prisoners."

"Yes," he went on, "they let me out yesterday afternoon. I caught the morning steamer to the island."

She was near enough to see the heavy moustache, the thin pinched face in which dark eyes glowed in their sunken sockets.

154

He was very much changed from the gay, reckless happy-go-lucky young man she had known only a year ago.

He laughed again.

"Believe it or not nobody on the steamer recognised me," he declared. "I must admit I kept well out of the way of the other passengers. When I came ashore I walked to the farm. I didn't meet anybody on the way."

Suddenly he put out his arms and drew her to him. He kissed her fiercely, but, when she did not respond, he drew back suddenly.

"You don't seem too pleased to see me," he muttered, looking down into her face. She had not responded to his kiss.

"I am, Mark!" she said. "It—it's just been such a shock—"

"You didn't write," he accused, and added in a different tone, "Not even to say you wanted to give me up."

Her heart was racing. What could she say or do? Did he expect that, in spite of her silence, she still loved him?

What would her father say if he heard

that Mark had come here to the farm rather than to the castle?

Would he forbid him the house? As the Laird would surely do if Mark presented himself at the castle.

He was watching her closely as these thoughts flashed through her mind.

"Well?" he asked at last.

Suddenly she cried passionately, all the frustration, the grief and despair she had felt during the past year, in her voice:

"Oh, Mark, why did you do it? Why did you get mixed up with those awful people?"

He turned from her and looked out across the stackyard, bright in the morning sun.

"I was bored, Fiona. Grandfather kept me under his thumb. If I did everything he wanted me to do, it was OK. If I strayed one inch from the narrow path he was down on me like a ton of bricks. I admit now I was a fool, not only because of what I did, but because I allowed myself to be so easily picked up by the police. Men I trusted let me down. They got away with it; I didn't!"

Fiona could hear no trace of shame in his voice, no hint of regret. He considered he had been unlucky, the victim of circumstances. That was all.

He swung round again and took her hand.

"I've put the past behind me now, Fiona. I'm going to make a fresh start— with you."

He drew her towards him. His eyes glowed as they met hers.

She felt hypnotised by those eyes. She longed to break free and run for it. But her legs refused to move.

"While I was in prison a chap told me about a business he's going to start when he's out in a month's time," he said. "It's in London. He wants me to go in with him. Second-hand cars."

An ex-convict dealing in cars—Fiona thought she knew what that meant!

"There's plenty of money in it, love," Mark continued. "We could be happy away from Bleiside, away from that miserable old man shut up in his godforsaken castle."

"But—he's your grandfather, Mark!"

The words came from stiff lips. Her voice sounded high-pitched, unnatural in her own ears.

"He'll never forgive me," Mark said harshly. "I know him better than anybody else. No! I realised when I went to prison that my time on Bleiside was at an end. The old man left me in no doubt that he'd disinherit me. In any case, I've had a taste of the outside world, and that's where my place is—not shut away in a crazy old castle on a tin-pot island in the back of beyond."

She opened her mouth to speak, to tell him she could never go away from the island with him, could never leave her father, all she loved, behind her.

But before she could say anything a voice sounded from the sunny stackyard:

"Who's this, Fiona?"

It was her father. He must have decided he was fit enough to leave his bed. He had dressed and come seeking her. He leaned heavily on his stick as he looked at Mark's back.

Mark turned and faced him. His eyes were narrowed as they looked at the older man.

"Don't you recognise me, Mr. Campbell? Have I changed so very much?"

"Mark Murray!" Hamish Campbell gasped. "But—I thought . . ."

"You thought I was still in prison, eh? Well, believe it or not, I was a good boy and they let me out a little bit earlier than expected. Prisons are pretty crowded these days. They needed my cell."

"And you came here imagining my girl would still be waiting for you?"

"Something like that. I've just been telling her my plans for the future—our future."

Mr. Campbell looked at Fiona.

"You surely don't still love him!" he cried.

His face was pale. His hand on the stick trembled.

She pushed past Mark and put her arm round him. She looked into his face.

"No, Daddy, I don't still love him," she said in a low voice. "I stopped loving him a long time ago."

"Then you'd better go, Mark," her father said, cold eyes on the young man. "You forfeited a decent girl's love when you behaved so disgracefully."

Mark's face twisted in rage. He raised his fist as if he would strike the older man. Fiona stepped in front of her father. Her face was defiant.

"Don't be so stupid, Mark," she exclaimed.

"You mean you think you can throw me aside—like an old coat?" Mark sneered. His voice rose, "What's happened to all those sweet words and passionate promises when I asked you to marry me? They must have meant something."

"They did—then! But no more. I'm sorry, Mark. It's over." She shook her head. "It wasn't just a youthful prank. It was a vicious crime. I could never forget it. You must see that."

She heard a little whimper of sound behind and turned to look at her father. His eyes were closed. His face was colourless. He was swaying helplessly.

"Daddy!"

She put her arm round him. She began to lead him towards the farmhouse.

"I—I must lie down," he muttered.

"I'll get you indoors," she said, then cried out: "Jessie! Jessie!"

The housekeeper heard her frightened call and came running from the house. Together the two women supported the sick man to the door of the building.

Before they went inside Fiona glanced over her shoulder. Murray was striding away towards the road. He did not look back.

13

AFTER breakfast Jean went up to her room. Andrew had said little during the meal. Adam had sensed that something was wrong and had tried to ease the strain by telling a story of one of his London clients who had made a will leaving a fortune to a dog. The young English couple had laughed dutifully.

The Laird and his daughter did not come down to breakfast so the three young people had the big dining room to themselves.

Suddenly Andrew pushed his chair back.

"I'm going to the library," he said abruptly, and hurried from the room.

The young solicitor looked at Jean.

"Anything wrong?" he asked gently.

"No, nothing," she said with false brightness and followed Andrew's example and went from the room.

Adam smiled grimly to himself. Of course there was something wrong. Everyone on the island knew that! He had hoped he might help.

Jean stood by the bedroom window and looked out. The sun was shining but over the far islands dark clouds were gathering.

Was that a storm in the offing? she wondered. Adam had told her yesterday that a pleasant day could be transformed into a black and stormy one with rough seas and gale force winds in a matter of minutes.

There came a tap at the door. It was Mrs. Baird. Her genial face wore an apologetic expression.

"The Laird would like to see you in his room," she said.

"In his study?" Jean asked.

The woman shook her head.

"No, in his bedroom," the other replied. "It's the first door on the left beyond the top of the staircase."

Jean was puzzled by this unusual summons. Why did the Laird want to see her in his bedroom? Did he think there was less chance of interruption than if he had sent for her to his study?

Her first impulse was to ignore the summons; then she decided that would be foolish. However hostile his intentions to her might be, the Laird was her fiancé's grandfather and her host. If he sent for her she should at least go and see what he wanted.

Her heart quickened as she went along the corridor and halted outside the old man's door.

She raised her hand and knocked.

"Come in!" the deep voice called and she turned the handle and went into the big bedroom.

A four-poster bed stood against one oak-panelled wall. The mahogany wardrobe looking out of place against the oak panels, and the many mirrored dressing table were at right angles on the opposite side of the room. A table stood before the tall window and seated at this table, a breakfast tray before him, was the Laird.

He rose as she entered the room. He

was wearing a heavy quilted dressing gown. A silk scarf tied at his neck.

"Good morning, my dear," he said affably. "Come and sit down."

She was surprised at the warmth of her reception. Since she had arrived at Arachnock Castle with Andrew he had treated her coldly—when he had noticed her at all.

Suspiciously she took the chair he indicated. He stroked his beard and regarded her in silence for several seconds.

"You are in love with my grandson?" he asked.

"I'm engaged to be married to him," she said a trifle sharply.

"That isn't necessarily the same thing," he said. "I asked you if you loved him."

"Yes, of course I love him. That is why I said I would marry him!"

She wondered what he was getting at. She did not trust him. There was something behind his questioning which so far she did not understand.

"When a woman loves a man she is usually prepared to make sacrifices for his happiness," the old man went on; "You agree?"

"Yes, of course."

Her heart sank. For the first time she realised why he had sent for her.

"I sent for Adam Simmonds to visit me because I intended to have him draw up another will for me," the old man said. "In certain circumstances I shall name Andrew as my heir. He will replace Mark, my other grandson."

When she did not speak he went on:

"When I die Andrew, as my heir, will become Laird of Arachnock Castle, owner of Bleiside Island. He will be a rich man, a great landowner, possessor of a famous name." He paused. "Do you think that would appeal to him?" he asked ironically.

"I'm not the person to answer that question, Mr. Murray," she said.

"I think you are! You know him better than I do. After all, he asked you to marry him."

She drew a deep breath. Facing him bravely, brown eyes a-fire, she said:

"You mentioned that you would make Andrew your heir, 'in certain circumstances'. What exactly are those circumstances?"

He opened a box on the table before him and took out a thin cigar. He did not answer her question until he had lit the cigar and blown a cloud of smoke towards the high ceiling of the big room. The smoke hung heavily in the air, forming lazy patterns.

"Let me tell you about another young English girl who came to this island long ago," he said, fixing her with his cold grey eyes. "She must have been a little younger than you, I imagine, but as pretty as you are. She married my son."

He regarded the burning tip of his cigar.

"At first they were happy enough, but the life on Bleiside Island did not suit her. She, like you, grew up in an English town. She missed its comforts."

He said the word "comforts" with a snap of his thin lips.

"Soon she and my son were quarrelling.

My son began to drink too much. He neglected his duties. A baby came. It made little difference."

He shook cigar ash into a heavy glass ash tray on which the family crest was engraved. His heavy brows were drawn down in a frown.

"Then one night my son was killed. He drove his car into a tree. He was drunk. That ill-fated marriage was at an end. His wife left Bleiside the day after the funeral. I never saw her again."

"But you have seen her son again," she said softly.

"Yes. I sent for him when my other grandson disgraced me by dragging the name of Murray through the mud. It is not often a man regains, as an adult, a chance in life which he lost as an infant. I waited . . . eagerly for my grandson to arrive at the castle."

"And you were disappointed once again," Jean murmured. "I came with him, the girl he told you he was to marry."

He nodded. He did not speak for some

168

time. Jean realised that, insofar as he was capable of gentleness, he was trying to express his wishes as gently as possible.

"You want me to tell Andrew he need not marry me?"

"You're a sensible girl," he said. "By insisting on Andrew making you his wife you would end his chance of becoming Laird of Arachnock. He would go back to the life you are familiar with—to be a petty clerk selling beans. It would not, I think, be an easy choice for him to make."

"You would disinherit him because you do not agree with him marrying me—and living here at the castle, with me?"

"It's not exactly a question of disinheritance yet, is it? But yes. I don't want my own son's tragic marriage to be repeated. Life on Bleiside Island would be very different from the life you'd been used to. Andrew might settle down—I believe he would—but you wouldn't. Soon enough you would long for the city, for all the things you've been used to all your life, which cannot be had here. Go away, my dear. Spare yourself a great deal of unhappiness, and ensure that Andrew's future as the head of a great family is safe."

Observing Jean's fierce resentment, he added: "Don't forget, my dear, that when I decided that Andrew should be my heir I had no idea he was engaged to be married."

"And suppose Andrew *prefers* to marry me, prefers the life he knows to being Laird of Arachnock?"

"It wouldn't be long before he began to realise what he had missed. I fear he'd blame you. Make no mistake of that. When money was tight—if, perhaps he lost his job—he'd think of what might have been. Do you believe"—he gave her a penetrating glance—"his love for you would overcome that?"

She stood up. Something told her he was right. How deep was their love? Till now, it had never been tested. Now, she felt, if she and Andrew married and they fell on hard times—perhaps even without that—Andrew would brood over what he might have been if he hadn't married her.

His behaviour over the last two days made her certain of that.

But she wasn't going to give in so easily. She met the eyes under the heavy brows.

"You'd better talk to Andrew," she said, striving to keep her voice steady. "If he wants to marry me and return to our house in Baston then that will be good enough for me. If he says he prefers to give me up and do as you say—well, I'll go away at once."

He stood up and came round the table. He took her hand.

"Thank you, my dear," he said. "You're a sensible girl. I felt sure you would take the most sensible course."

She pulled her hand roughly out of his and made for the door. Tears threatened and she didn't want him to see them.

Downstairs she hesitated in the hall. Andrew looked out of the library.

"Oh, there you are! I thought you must have gone out for another walk. There's not much else to do here, I must admit."

She went into the book-lined room and stood looking down into the fire.

"Your grandfather sent for me," she said. "He wants me to go away. He says if we go ahead and get married he'll send you away from the castle. Your chance of being his heir will be at an end!"

He stared at her with shocked eyes.

"But he *wants* to make me his heir! He said so!"

"He thinks you'll regret it if you marry me. He may be right."

"How can you say that! He knows I love you!"

Peter's protest seemed unconvincing. She turned and looked at him.

"Are you sure you do? Would you really give up all this"—she looked round the big room—"just to marry me and go back to that supermarket?"

A shadow crossed his face. He avoided meeting her gaze.

"It's all so unfair," he muttered. "Why should the old man be so unfair? Why shouldn't we get married and I still be Laird of Arachnock?"

172

"I think I know why," she said quietly. "He has someone else in mind for you."

He frowned. "Good God, who?" he demanded.

"Fiona Campbell," she replied. "We know he's determined to own all Bleiside Island and that only Mr. Campbell stands in his way. With me out of the way in London he'd soon encourage you to seek out Fiona. After all, she's a very pretty girl, the only one on the island I should think, and with Mark in prison and out of the running, she'd soon turn to you— if you encouraged her."

"I never heard such nonsense!" he blustered. "If he's thinking like that, I've a good mind to take the next steamer back to the mainland."

"I don't believe you really mean that, Andrew," she said quietly. She crossed to the door. "I'm going to my room. I'll put my things together and ask the chauffeur to take me into the village to wait for the afternoon steamer."

He stared after her but she stopped him with a gesture.

173

"Don't make it any harder, Andrew," she begged. "It's perhaps better this way."

Out in the hall she stood for a moment fighting back her tears. In spite of what she had said, she hoped, even now, that Andrew would follow her, take her into his arms and tell her that never, never would he give her up, that he loved her far better than any thought of being Laird of Arachnock. But she knew he had made up his mind.

Then she lifted her chin and made for the stairs, her face set and determined. She had told Andrew it was better this way, and in her heart of hearts she believed it was.

He had never really loved her. They had been thrown together, two young people, rather lonely, who found they liked each other—the progress from friendship to love had been easy and inevitable. She couldn't remember that Andrew had ever asked her to marry him in so many words. It had simply become an accepted decision after a time.

Neither of them had known much excitement in their lives. They had enjoyed meeting on Saturday mornings to look for furniture for the little house they had hoped to buy. But their prospects had not been exciting.

Then Angus Murray and Arachnock Castle had entered their lives. Overnight, everything was completely changed.

Andrew's reaction was understandable, especially if (as Jean suspected) he already felt attracted by Fiona Campbell. If he had never heard of Arachnock Castle, never met the Campbell girl, then he might have settled down quite happily with Jean. Now, he never could, whatever happened.

She reached her door and stopped with her hand on the doorknob. The thought struck her that her own feelings for Andrew had changed. If she were really honest with herself, did she still want to settle down with Andrew as they had planned?

And did she really love Andrew as much as she had thought? If she had, would a chance encounter with a man in a train make her heart jump, as it had when she first looked up into the smiling eyes of Adam Simmonds?

14

MARK'S mother had two rooms in a tower which rose above the battlements at one corner of the castle.

She had been living in these isolated apartments ever since Mark had been sent to prison.

They were approached from the first floor by a spiral staircase. There was also a flight of stone steps outside which led above the sea to a tiny balcony.

Once the tower had been a look-out for those keeping watch over the sea approaches for any enemy from the mainland. Its isolation suited Morag Anderson.

When her son had disgraced himself the Laird, her father, had left her in no doubt that his feelings towards Mark extended to her as well.

She tried to defend the son she loved; but her father would have none of it.

"He's shamed us all," was all he would say. "Don't mention his name to me again. From now on he does not exist. I must look elsewhere for an heir."

So Morag Anderson had shut herself away at the back of the castle emerging only for meals, and when she was overwhelmingly lonely, to talk to Mrs. Baird, who ran the household. For the most part she ignored her father, and he made little effort to restore relations.

Her loneliness combined with the shock of her son's disgrace had led perhaps inevitably to a nervous breakdown. The Laird—advised by the doctor—had sent her to a nursing home on the mainland. After six weeks she had been discharged and had returned to the island. She had nowhere else to go.

The specialist had written to the Laird and told him that, in his opinion, Mrs. Anderson was hardly fit to be alone. He had only released her with the greatest reluctance. She was mentally disturbed and should, in his view, be carefully watched for several weeks to come. He had emphasised the importance of weekly checkups, but Morag Anderson had not kept the appointments.

The Laird had ignored this. If Morag was happier at home, living her own strange isolated life, so be it. He would not force her to do anything she did not want to do.

Mark knew nothing of his mother's condition. When he had been sent to prison he had, during the first three months of his sentence, received letters from her.

After that—nothing. He had written to her twice but had had no reply. He had assumed that, probably influenced by her father, she had decided to shut him out of her life.

This morning, when he left the Campbell farm after discovering that Fiona had no welcome for him, he had walked along the shore, angry and frustrated.

He supposed he ought to have helped Fiona with her father when the old man collapsed. But Mr. Campbell had left him in no doubt that, like all the others, he hated and distrusted him, so he had turned and hurried away.

Ahead of him looming against the darkening sky on its isolated headland stood the grim stony bulk of Arachnock Castle.

"My inheritance," he thought bitterly, and knew that it was an inheritance he would never enjoy.

He knew his grandfather. When the Laird had banished him from the castle that had been the end of his chances of ever living on Bleiside Island again.

"Not that I want to," he thought, looking round at the desolate moors, at the windswept shore. "I learned a great deal in prison, the most important being that there's a big world out there"—he looked out to sea—"full of opportunities for someone who has his wits about him."

He grinned to himself. It was surprising what you learned during a year in gaol.

He knew what he must do. He had very little money. The first thing was to get enough to cover his living expenses over the next few months.

After that, London would be his destination. He had plenty of friends there. With a little capital he would soon be on the up and up.

He started along the beach again. Presently he drew near to the castle. The tide was out and he had no difficulty scrambling over the rocks and reaching the steep walls which rose like a cliff above him.

He remembered how, as a boy, he had often climbed up the castle walls to the balcony above. Over the centuries the elements had partly worn away the blocks of stone and provided precarious hand and foot holds for an active lad.

Further along the shore, beyond the first barrier of rocks, there was an overhang which made climbing the cliff face impossible, as Jean had found out the day before.

Mark started to climb. Presently he was swinging himself over the railings which guarded the balcony which ran round the castle. He stood for a few moments looking out to sea.

A storm was building up; there could be no doubt about that. Heavy black clouds hung over the sea and a mist, which he knew was rain, was already shrouding the outer islands.

He had remembered something his mother had said in one of her letters.

"I am going to live by myself in the old watchtower," she had written. "Your grandfather has little patience with me. I prefer to be alone."

He made for the door which led into the castle. He tip-toed past the kitchen, where Mrs. Baird could be heard banging pots and pans, to the little spiral staircase which led up to his mother's rooms. Half a minute later he was tapping at the door at the top.

At first there was no response to his knocking, then a scared white face looked out at him from a narrow lancet in the wall beside the door.

"Mum, let me in!" Mark said.

Her face lit up. Her nervous hands

juggled with a key. She unlocked the door and threw it open.

"Mark!"

They were in each other's arms. Tears ran down her pale cheeks. She held him tight as if she never meant to let him go.

At last he pulled her gently away.

"Let's go inside," he said, and pulled the door to behind them.

They crossed to two chairs set before a smouldering peat fire. Even in summer, fires were needed to warm the thick stone walls of the castle. Mark sank into a chair and smiled up at his mother.

"You didn't expect to see me, eh?"

She shook her head.

"I can't believe it! I—I thought. . . ?"

"You thought I'd still some weeks to go. But they'd forgotten to allow for time spent in custody under arrest. He gave a hard harsh laugh. "The prisons are over-crowded. They were glad to see the back of me."

"And you came—home?"

Her eyes were glowing with happiness. She at least had not rejected him. She went down on her knees before him and took his hands.

"Oh, Mark, it seems such a long time since you went away. And now you're back!"

"I'm not staying, Mum," he said. "I don't want the old man to know I'm here, either. Do you hear?"

Her eyes flashed.

"But why not? You belong here! You're the rightful heir to Arachnock!"

"I'm not any longer and you know it, Mum. Grandfather left me in no doubt about that before I was taken away. He didn't actually say 'Don't darken my doors again!' but he meant it and you must realise it. In any case, he said enough to make me quit this place whether he wants me to or not."

A cunning look came into Morag Anderson's thin face.

"You mustn't give up too easily, my love!" she whispered. He looked at her curiously.

The old girl has changed, he decided. There was something strange about her.

Gone was the cool reserved woman he had known since childhood, the woman who had ruled the castle with a rod of iron.

Now there was something almost childish about her, a twitch at the corner of her mouth, a strange look in her eyes. Surely she couldn't be going senile at her age?

"Your grandfather has brought someone else to the castle to take your place," she muttered, plucking at the sleeve of his jacket. "He's the son of my brother and the woman who went away after your uncle was killed."

Mark frowned. So the old man had tracked down the cousin he had only heard about, the son of his dead uncle who had been taken away from the island when he was only a baby. He had only been a child himself then. His grandfather had always led him to believe that he would inherit Arachnock until he had that bad bit of luck with the police which landed him in prison.

"You must stay here, Mark," his mother went on. "No one need know you are here in the watch-tower. I'll bring you food. We'll make up a bed for you—"

He shook his head at this absurd, pathetic suggestion.

"I'm not staying, Mum," he said. "I have other plans, plans which don't include Arachnock Castle or Bleiside Island."

She stared at him bewildered.

"But you must stay! You belong here!"

"I came to ask you to let me have some money, Mum," he said quietly. "I don't want to stay. My life is in England, in London. I can do well there—better than if I stayed in this hole. I only need a little capital—"

She began to shake. He gripped her hands tightly to steady her.

"You must stay, you must!" she cried shrilly. "You are the rightful heir to Arachnock! The impostor will be sent away and you will resume your rightful place."

Her voice rose to a scream. He put his hand over her mouth to stifle the mad sound. Her eyes glared into his as he held her.

"Be quiet!" he snapped. "Do you want to bring them all running to see what's going on?"

He held her till she was quieter. She was crying now, a thin wailing sound.

"You'll stay?" she begged. "For one night, at least?"

He nodded. It was obvious if he was to get anything out of her he would have to humour her for a while.

"Yes, I'll stay," he promised. "Later, we'll have another talk."

She nodded. The look she gave him frightened him. What was wrong with her? he wondered. She acted like a crazy woman.

"Yes, we'll have another talk," she muttered. "A long, long talk."

15

THE steamer normally called at Bleiside Island in the middle of the afternoon. Jean had planned to meet it then and return to the mainland.

But by lunch time the weather had turned so bad she wondered if the boat would sail. Rain was falling heavily and a rising wind had turned the waters of the sound into a maelstrom. Already, though the tide was only just on the turn, huge waves were crashing against the cliff above which the castle towered. Spray carried on the wind partly obscured the view from the bedroom window at which Jean stood looking gloomily out at the storm.

She had packed her few clothes in her hold-all and had been sitting in the room since after breakfast, and that decisive conversation with Andrew, which seemed to have settled their future.

She had no wish to see either Andrew or the Laird again. She was consumed with a desire to leave the castle as quickly as possible, to go back to Baston and pick up the threads of her old life.

As the slow hours of the morning dragged by she found herself wondering if Andrew would, even now, try to dissuade her from returning to England. But he did not come, and by eleven o'clock she knew for certain that he never would.

"He's really glad I'm going home," she told herself, "even if he can't admit it to my face. He realises it is the best solution for both of us."

But her heart was aching as she stood at the window looking out over the stormy sea. They had been happy, untroubled. It was hard to accept that the future, which had been so bright with promise, was now a dark tunnel through which she must walk alone.

A knock sounded on the door. In spite of herself and her earlier resolutions her heart rose.

So Andrew had come to see her, after all.

She opened the door. Adam Simmonds was looking in at her.

"Andrew told me half an hour ago that you are hoping to return to the mainland on the afternoon steamer," he said, his handsome face concerned.

She nodded. "Yes, I am. I must ask the Laird's chauffeur to run me into Bleiside."

He shook his head.

"The steamer won't be calling at the island. The weather's too rough. I was hoping to catch it for I'm returning to London with the Laird's will. Now it looks as if we'll have to wait until tomorrow."

Her face fell.

"Oh, but I can't stay here another night," she said wildly. "I—I—"

He took a step towards her and laid a steadying hand on her arm.

"Easy!" he murmured. "It may be a blessing in disguise. Both you and

190

Andrew will have another chance to talk things over."

"There's nothing to talk over! The Laird as good as asked me to leave the castle and Andrew apparently prefers being the heir of Arachnock to being my husband!"

Her voice was bitter. He saw the angry tears that had filled her eyes.

"I'm sure the Laird will grow to love you if you hold out and marry Andrew. Anyone would!" He spoke with strong convictions.

"But he says he'll disinherit Andrew if he marries me. Besides, Andrew doesn't want to marry me," she said.

"Are you quite sure of that? When I was talking to him half an hour ago he seemed very confused."

She laughed sharply.

"He hasn't shown much interest in me since I spoke to him after breakfast, when I told him I was leaving." She looked at him, sudden suspicion in her glance. "He —he hasn't sent you up here to talk to me, has he?"

Adam's jaw tightened. He avoided her eyes, and seemed suddenly uncomfortable.

"He left the castle a few minutes ago," he said quietly. "Douggie MacLean came back from doing some shopping in Bleiside with the news that Fiona Campbell's father has had a heart attack. Andrew set off at once for the Campbell farm." He added: "It sounds serious.'

"I'm sorry about Mr. Campbell," Jean said. "I suppose," she went on a bit ruefully, "I suppose Andrew felt Fiona needed a friend with her at such a time."

She turned back to the spray-drenched window. The thought suddenly struck her how much happier she would be at this moment if she had come to Arachnock castle with Adam instead of Andrew. How much happier everyone would be!

She heard the door close quietly and looked round. Adam had gone from the room. Jean felt a sudden longing for him to come back.

Andrew battled his way along the road in

192

the teeth of the gale, which whipped his hair back from his scalp and tore the very breath out of his mouth.

As soon as he had heard that Fiona's father had had a heart attack he had known he must be with her.

If Mr. Campbell died Fiona would more than ever need a friend by her side.

He glanced guiltily over his shoulder. Arachnock Castle reared, black and forbidding, against the stormy sky.

He wondered what Jean was thinking at that moment. When she had left him in the library he had been tempted to go after her, tempted to take her in his arms and tell her that nothing—nothing!— must ever come between them, that he would return to England with her, that he would put his grandfather and his plans to make him his heir out of his mind.

But he'd stayed where he was. Somehow he couldn't bring himself to reject this wonderful opportunity that had opened up for him. Laird of Arachnock Castle! Surely, no one, least of all Jean, could expect him to reject such a future out of hand.

Rather sulkily he had stayed in the library until news had come of Mr. Campbell's heart attack. Then he had forgotten everything in the conviction that he must get to Fiona's side at once, to comfort her, to stand by her in her trouble . . .

He was breathless, exhausted by his battle against the gale when, at last, he turned off the road and made his way down the track to the farm.

A car was standing outside the kitchen door. He knocked, then, not waiting for a reply, opened the door and went into the house.

Jessie Mackenzie was standing by the kitchen fire. She was staring into the flames. She did not seem to have heard Andrew's knock, nor to be aware that he had entered the house.

"Where—where's Fiona?" he demanded.

She turned slowly towards him, showing no surprise at his presence in the kitchen. He saw that her eyes were full of tears.

"The puir lassie," she whispered. "She loved her father so!"

He went through into the hall beyond. He found Fiona with a short middle-aged man who did not look round as he entered. Fiona was pale and composed. She seemed surprised to see him.

"Fiona—I heard your father had been taken ill," he blurted out, suddenly not sure that he should have come.

"He died half an hour ago," she said quietly. "This is Dr. Gordon. He was with my father when he died."

"I'm so sorry!"

An uncertain little smile of gratitude flickered for a moment across her pretty face.

The doctor looked at her with concern. "I'll be on my way, Fiona," he said. "I'll look in later." He patted her on the arm gently.

Giving Andrew a nod, he hurried from the room. Andrew crossed to Fiona's side and took her hand.

"If there's anything I can do . . ." he said uncertainly.

She looked at him as if she was seeing him for the first time.

"She's in shock," he thought. "She can't believe it's happened. Soon enough she'll realise. That's when she'll need me."

She looked up at him like a wide-eyed child.

"It was so sudden," she whispered. "He—he lay there, eyes closed, then—then suddenly he opened them, tried to speak—and died."

He drew her into the shelter of his arms. Holding her close with one arm he put up his other hand to stroke her soft silky hair.

"There, there!" he murmured. "He must have gone peacefully. And he had you by his side, you the daughter he loved."

She clung to him. Her tears flowed and she sobbed bitterly.

"We've—we've been everything to

each other—since my mother died," she said brokenly. "Now—I'm alone."

He shook his head.

"You're not alone," he told her. "You'll never be alone again."

She looked up into his face, soft mouth trembling, tear-filled eyes puzzled.

"I—I don't understand—"

He forgot everything then but that this girl needed him, that she meant more to him than anything else in the world.

"I'll take care of you," he murmured. "You see, Fiona, I know now that I love you. There can never be anybody else."

"But—that other girl—?"

He kissed her then, his mouth stifling the questions she would have asked.

And as his lips covered hers, she put her arms round his neck in a gesture of trust and clung to him.

Bewildered, even astonished, though she was, new hope was springing to life in her heart. The future no longer frightened her. A miracle had happened . . .

It was afternoon before Andrew left

Fiona. There had been so much to do, so much to discuss.

He had been able to help her with some of the sad duties that must be attended to after anyone dies. The doctor had returned with the death certificate and the news that he had spoken to an undertaker who would attend to the formalities that must be carried out before the funeral at the tiny Kirk in Bleiside in three days time.

When he left the farm the wind had dropped and Andrew made his way along the shore towards the castle. The doctor had told him that the afternoon steamer across the sound had been cancelled which meant that Jean would still be at the castle.

Andrew's heart sank at the thought of the coming interview with her. He must tell her about Fiona, how he now realised that it was Fiona, not Jean, he loved.

An unworthy thought came into his mind. If the steamer had called at the island, Jean would have already gone and he would not have had to confront her. It would have been so much easier to write to her.

Now he must face her . . .

As he approached the castle he felt he would like to put off seeing Jean for a little while longer. He had not ordered his thoughts. He was still bemused at the changes that had taken place so suddenly in his life.

He walked past the slope that led up to the castle and continued up the road. Presently he saw a path which he saw must lead to the cliff top.

He felt he would like to stand facing the sea, the cold rain in his face, staring out over the turbulent waves which, at the moment, matched his mood.

Soon he was standing at the cliff edge, the angry sea pounding the rocks directly below him.

How long he stood there he did not know. Neither did he realise that he was being watched. He never saw the dark figure which stole up behind him so silently, soft footfalls soundless above the whining of the wind and the crash of the waves on the rocks below.

Morag Anderson had seen Andrew walking on the shore. She had gone out on to the balcony outside the watch-tower window to watch him.

Hatred filled her heart. This was the man who had deprived her own son of his birthright. If only there was some way she could drive him away from Bleiside. Once he had gone her father would then be forced to change his mind and make her own son his heir again.

"Come in, mother!" Mark called from the room behind. "You'll catch your death of cold out there."

She went inside and closed the window behind her. Mark was sprawled in an armchair before the fire, a glass of whisky in his hand. He looked half asleep.

He did not look up when she crossed to the door. She went down the short flight of stairs that led to the upper corridor which would take her to the main staircase.

At the top she stood looking into the hall below. Her nephew would soon come into sight for he must be approaching the castle entrance now.

But when he did not appear she went downstairs, frowning. He must have gone on past the castle. It was wild weather for a walk but perhaps he preferred to be out in the wind and the rain rather than cooped up in the castle.

She went down to the hall, snatched a cape from a cupboard under the stairs. Pulling it about her, she stepped out into the courtyard and down the track leading from the castle.

Out on the road, there was no sight of Andrew.

Where could he be? she wondered. He had come from the direction of Bleiside so, as he wasn't in sight, he must have gone further up the road.

Yet from where she stood the road stretched in an almost straight line for nearly half a mile. Andrew would still be in sight if he had gone that way.

Suddenly she realised that he must have

turned aside to take the path leading to the top of the cliff.

She hurried along the road, and climbed the path up which Andrew had walked a few minutes before. She saw him standing at the edge of the cliff. She knew what she must do.

It was for her son's sake, she told herself. Often enough she felt confused, bewildered; but not now. Her mind was as clear as crystal.

This man was a thief. He was stealing her beloved son's heritage. He must be swept aside.

Stealthily she approached the unsuspecting man at the edge of the cliff.

He turned and saw her even as she lunged at him. He flung out and down, trying to save himself—but he was too late.

With a startled shout he disappeared over the edge of the cliff.

16

ANDREW was conscious of a severe pain in his right shoulder. He groaned as he tried to sit up. Where was he?

There was the thunderous sound of the sea below him. A high wind blew in his face. He felt bitterly cold.

He wondered how long he had been unconscious. He began to remember what had happened. The figure sneaking up on him, outstretched arms which thrust at him as he stood at the edge of the cliff, a glimpse of the mad face of a woman as she watched him disappear from sight.

"I should be on the rocks below," he thought and shuddered.

He tried to sit up then almost cried out with agony of the movement. He must have broken his arm when he had landed on the ledge which was evidently close under the cliff above.

He looked around. Behind was the steep face of the cliff. A few inches from where he lay was the sheer drop to the sea below.

One unwise movement and he would roll off the ledge. He must lie perfectly still and decide what to do.

Yet what could he do? Obviously he could not climb the smooth face of the cliff even if he hadn't broken his arm. And the chance of anyone coming along the cliff top and discovering his plight was very, very unlikely. Even if someone did come that way they were not likely to look over the edge and see him.

As for the drop below, there was no escape that way either. He tried not to think what would have happened if his falling body had missed the ledge and he had fallen on to the sea-washed rocks at the foot of the cliff.

Cautiously he tried to find a more comfortable position for his injured arm. He cried out in pain as he moved. In spite of the cold he felt a sweat of agony break out on his forehead.

He must have lost consciousness again for when next he opened his eyes the wind had dropped and darkness was creeping over the sea . . .

Jean had spent most of the day in her room. It faced away from the village of Bleiside and the Campbell's farm and afforded her a rather dismal view of cliff top and desolate moorland.

Mrs. Baird had come up at mid-day to ask if she would be going down to lunch. But Jean had said she preferred to stay where she was. She had no wish to meet the Laird. She had little doubt that Andrew would stay at the Campbell farm with Fiona, it was becoming quite clear to her that the Laird's plan in that respect had turned out successfully. She was surprised at the equanimity with which she could face the fact that Andrew loved someone else.

The housekeeper had brought up a tray of sandwiches and a pot of coffee, and after the meal Jean had lain down on the bed. If she could get to sleep it would help pass the hours which must elapse before she could leave Bleiside Island for ever . . .

But although she did not want to see Angus Murray or his grandson, she was hoping that the other English visitor to Arachnock Castle might look in to see her. When she shut her eyes, it was the strong, reserved face of Adam Simmonds that she saw.

She had an instinct that Adam's feelings towards her were more than mere sympathetic interest. But he had not said or done anything which could give her real hope. Their situation was difficult. After all, she was still officially engaged to Andrew.

When the tapping came, she knew it was Adam before she opened the door. He smiled at her in an inquiring way.

"I wondered if you were feeling unwell," he said.

"No, thank you. A bit tired. I want to be alone for a while."

Adam at once made as if to go, but she stopped him with a hand on his arm. Her

206

large soft eyes gazed up at the tall figure of the young solicitor.

"It was kind of you—" she began.

Adam felt a sudden desire to take this vulnerable creature into his arms and comfort her. His natural caution—he was not a lawyer for nothing—restrained him. By being in her bedroom, alone with her, he was already committing a grave breach of etiquette.

Perhaps tomorrow, when both of them would be leaving this wretched island, there would be a chance to talk freely. For all he knew she was as much in love with Andrew as ever she was. His spirit quailed when he thought that if, as he longed to do, he kissed her, she would think he was trying to take advantage of her. The poor child had enough troubles already.

"I'd better go," he said.

She nodded, and smiled a rather watery little smile.

Later Jean did manage to sleep though she was fully dressed. She must have been exhausted for when she awakened darkness was falling and someone was knocking at the door.

It was Mrs. Baird again. The housekeeper's rosy face was anxious.

"I came up earlier to see if you'd like a cup of tea, miss," she said. "But you were asleep and I hesitated to wake you. Will you be coming down for dinner a little later?"

"What time is it?" Jean asked, suppressing a yawn.

"Just after half-past six. Dinner's at seven."

Jean suddenly realised she was ravenously hungry. She had only eaten two of the sandwiches Mrs. Baird had brought for her lunch.

Suddenly she thought: "I don't see why I should go hungry because of Andrew. If I don't go down to dinner he'll think I'm afraid of him, or what is worse ashamed of myself! And that I can't allow."

"Yes, I'll come down," she told the housekeeper, and when the woman had gone she slipped off the bed and went to the window.

The gale had died down now. Although the wind was still blowing rain against the window it was nothing like the hurricane that had raged earlier.

She thrust open the window and leaned out. After the stuffiness of the room behind her the cold fresh air was a tonic.

She drew it in with pleasure. She decided that later, when dinner was over, she would go for a walk. It would be better than sitting over a fire in the castle library or sitting room.

She frowned, thinking she heard a faint call from the direction of the sea. When it was repeated she stayed listening, her hand on the window fastening.

Was it a seagull? she wondered. Yet there were no seagulls visible in the twilit sky.

Perhaps they were out of sight below the edge of the cliff. Even so they would almost certainly soar into view.

She had heard somewhere that they did not, as other sea birds did, nest on the ledges which nature had carved out of the cliff.

The cry was repeated. She frowned. It was not a seagull's cry, she was sure of that now. If it hadn't been so unlikely she would have said it was a human voice she had heard.

Someone knocked on the door. She ran to open it. Adam smiled in at her.

"Mrs. Baird says you're coming down to dinner," he said. "I'm so glad."

She took his arm and drew him across the room.

"Listen!" she said, indicating the open window.

He frowned and looked at her as if puzzled by her words.

"What's the matter?" he asked.

"There it is again!" she cried. "I'm sure there's someone out there calling for help."

He leaned out of the window as she had done earlier. At first there was nothing. Then the faint shout came again and Adam looked over his shoulder at the anxious girl.

"It certainly sounds as if someone needs help," he said, "though where they can be goodness only knows."

"Perhaps we'd better go out and investigate," she said.

"Put a coat on," he said practically. "And meet me in the hall."

He ran out of the room ahead of her. A minute later she joined him. He had pulled on an anorak. They left the castle together.

Douggie MacLean, the Laird's chauffeur, was outside, about to put the old Rolls away for the night in the garage at the far side of the courtyard.

"MacLean, we think there's someone in difficulty on the cliff," Adam told him. "If you've got a rope bring it along. We'll go ahead of you."

"Very good," the little man said.

Adam and Jean lost no time in finding the path Andrew had earlier taken to the edge of the cliff.

They reached the point not far from the spot where Andrew had stood looking out to sea. They stood listening. But no sound reached them. Whoever had called out was silent now.

They searched the top of the cliffs in the semi-darkness. Presently Douggie MacLean joined them, a coiled rope over his shoulder.

He went to the edge of the cliff and looked over. He turned to shout to Adam: "Mr. Simmonds, there's someone down there!"

Adam and Jean hurried to his side. Adam looked cautiously over.

Fifteen feet below a dark form was lying on a ledge.

"Hello, down there! Who are you?" he shouted.

There was silence except for the sound of the waves on the rocks far below. Adam shouted again.

This time a faint call came back.

"I've broken my arm! Can you help me?"

"It's Andrew," Jean gasped. "He must have been walking on the cliff and slipped over the edge."

"We must get him up," Adam said. "If

he makes an unwise move he'll slip off that ledge. It's too narrow for safety."

Jean shivered and not because of the cold wind.

"What can we do?" she whispered.

Adam looked at an outcrop of granite some way back from the edge of the cliff.

"If we can tie the rope around one of those boulders, I'll climb down to him," he said. "I'll stay with him to make sure he doesn't move and fall to his death while you get help from the Castle."

"It's the coastguards we'll be needing, sar," MacLean declared. "Perhaps the young lady would return to the castle and summon them."

"Yes, that's the best thing," Adam agreed, and looking at Jean: "Will you go back and tell the Laird what has happened? Tell him to ring the coast-guard station at Bleiside. They have proper equipment for situations like this."

She didn't want to leave him. If the rope broke under his weight, or the

213

boulder shifted, he would fall to his death. And she couldn't bear that.

Suddenly she realised that she was more anxious for his safety than for Andrew's!

"Hurry!" he said impatiently and turned to MacLean. "Come on, man! Let's get the rope tied around one of these boulders."

She delayed no longer. Without glancing at Adam again she ran across the open ground to the road. A minute later she was knocking on the Laird's study door and informing that astonished gentleman what was happening on the cliff top.

Andrew was conscious that someone was beside him on the ledge.

"Steady, old man!" a voice said when he tried to move.

He sank back against the cold face of the cliff with a groan. The pain in his arm was excruciating. He closed his eyes. He felt cold, almost at the end of his tether.

"It's Adam Simmonds," the voice said.

"You must hang on a while. Help will soon be coming."

"But—but how did you get down here to me?"

"A rope. I lowered myself to the ledge."

"How—how did you know I was down here?"

"Jean heard you shouting. It's a good job she had her room on that side of the castle or no one might have heard you."

I must keep him talking, Adam thought. If he loses consciousness and slumps forward I may not be able to hold him from falling into the sea.

"How did you come to fall over the cliff?" he asked.

Andrew's face hardened.

"I was pushed!" he said. "That devil of a woman pushed me."

Shocked, Adam exclaimed:

"What woman are you talking about?"

"My aunt. She hates me because I've taken her son's place as my grandfather's heir."

"But—surely she'd never do such a dreadful thing!"

"But I saw her—just for a split second." Andrew's voice rose excitedly. He stirred.

Adam pushed him gently back against the wall of the cliff.

"Steady, old man! I believe you. It must have been a terrible shock."

He was remembering something about Morag Anderson, how he had made arrangements some months ago at the Laird's request for her to go into a nursing home which specialised in mental cases.

She had seemed normal again when she had come back to the island. Apparently she had not been cured as he and the Laird had thought.

"She must have followed me on to the cliff," Andrew muttered. "I was standing at the edge. I half turned as she rushed at me, and for an instant I saw her face but I couldn't save myself. I suppose she thinks I must be lying on the rocks at this very moment."

He began to shake. Cautiously Adam slipped his arm about the trembling shoulders.

"Steady, there!" he said. "It won't be long before they come with some equipment to get us up to the top."

They waited in the darkness with the wind whining dismally and chilling them as it came off the sea, the cold rain adding to their discomfort.

Andrew seemed to be on the verge of losing consciousness. Adam concentrated on keeping him awake.

"The steamer didn't call at the island today so Jean couldn't go back to the mainland," he said.

Andrew roused himself with an effort.

"I know," he muttered.

"You're not going back with her, then?"

Andrew shook his head.

"No, I'm not! I'm staying here at—at Arachnock Castle. It's over between Jean and me."

Adam looked into the pale face. So the temptation to become the Laird's heir had been too much for Andrew Murray. He would rather give up the girl he was engaged to marry than miss the chance of being a rich man! Had he ever loved Jean as she deserved?

But it was really no business of his, he told himself. He would go back to London, prepare a new will for the Laird to sign and that would be the end of the business so far as he was concerned— unless Jean . . .

He heard a shout overhead. Looking up he saw heads silhouetted against the night sky, faces staring down at the ledge out of the gloom.

"They've come," he said. "Soon be safe now. Then we'll have to see about that arm."

17

MARK had been uneasy ever since his mother had returned to her rooms in the watch tower.

She was trembling. Her eyes were bright and excited. She walked about the room then stood looking intently out of the window as if something had caught her attention.

He went to her side.

"What is it, mother?" he asked. "Has something happened?"

Startled, she turned to him, shaking her head.

"No, nothing has happened," she muttered.

He felt uneasy. What was wrong with her? Her eyes were unfocussed. They stared beyond him rather than at him. There was a little smile on her lips, a strange smile that sent a shudder through him.

"Mum!" he said sharply. "What is it? What has happened?"

She turned back to the window to look out into the darkness. Only the after-glow of the dying day lay on the sea.

"You are your grandfather's heir," she said slowly. "He'll have to reconsider you now, Mark—now that interloper has gone."

"What are you talking about, Mum?" he demanded, and seizing her shoulders he turned her to face him.

There was a cunning look in her eyes and the same strange smile twisted her thin lips.

"Your grandfather must forgive you for what you did, Mark," she said. "He has no other heir than you. When he dies you will be Laird of Arachnock. There is nobody else."

He began to feel afraid. He had never seen her like this before. What had happened to change her? And what was all this about there being no other heir when his cousin, Andrew, was already living in the castle? Hadn't the old man made a will in his favour? So his mother had told him only a few hours before.

"Mother, what has happened? You went out earlier. Where?" He gave her a little shake. "Why are you telling me this about being my grandfather's heir? You know it's not true."

Slyly she said:

"But it is true, darling. You are the only heir, I promise you."

He let her go and went back to stare into the fire.

He had come to his mother to borrow money so he could go to London and start up in business. Now he was being told that his best interests were here on Bleiside where he would be reinstated as heir of Arachnock.

It must be nonsense. His grandfather had left him in no doubt when he went to prison that he never wanted to hear from him again. Nothing could make that old man change his mind.

Someone knocked on the outer door. Startled, Mark looked at his mother.

Nobody knew he was in the castle. It

would be best if they remained in ignorance.

"I'd better go into the bedroom," he said.

She nodded. She was still smiling that same secret smile.

"Yes, perhaps it would be as well," she agreed. "Soon it will not be necessary for you to hide. Soon you will walk proudly through the castle, your grandfather's true heir!"

The knock was repeated as he hurried into the bedroom. His mother made for the door and opened it.

The housekeeper was outside. Her face was redder than ever and there was an air of suppressed excitement about her.

"Oh, madam, there's been an accident," she said. "Mr. Andrew—they've just brought him back to the castle. He must have fallen down the cliff."

"What's that! What did you say, woman?"

Mrs. Anderson gripped the housekeeper's arm.

Mrs. Blair shook her head, surprised by the other's vehemence.

"Mr. Andrew must have slipped from the cliff edge," she replied. "Mercifully a ledge stopped his fall. He's broken his arm, by the looks of things. They've put him in his room and sent for the doctor."

When Mrs. Anderson did not speak she said:

"The Laird sent me to tell you. Thank God, the young man escaped with his life!"

Mrs. Anderson closed the door in the woman's face and went back to the sitting room. Mark opened the bedroom door and looked cautiously out.

"What was all that about?" he asked.

She turned to look at him. He gave a gasp of shock, for her face was twisted with rage.

"He's cheated me!" she mouthed. "He should have fallen to his death. Instead— the impostor is still alive!"

"Who are you talking about?" Mark demanded.

She was opening and closing her hands,

pressing the palms together and pulling at her fingers. There was a mad glare in her eyes.

"It's your cousin!" she cried, her voice rising. "He should have fallen to his death. They would have thought it was an accident. Instead—"

"Instead—what?" he asked and it was as if a cold hand had closed over his heart.

"Instead he'll tell them that he saw me. And they'll believe him! Your grandfather —my father—hates me. Your cousin and that girl hate me. Everybody hates me. They'll be glad to have something to torment me with!"

He moved to her side and hesitantly put his arm about her shoulders.

"Tell me what happened," he murmured.

Tears had now filled her stormy eyes. She clung to him as if she would never let him go.

"I thought if he was out of the way your grandfather would make you his heir again," she sobbed. "I thought—"

So that was where she must have gone

earlier, he realised. She had followed his cousin on to the cliff and had pushed him over. She had tried to murder him and only chance had saved Andrew.

If she had succeeded it would have been thought that Andrew had either been blown over the cliff edge or had gone too near and misjudging the distance, toppled to the sea below.

No one would ever have suspected he had been pushed to his death.

Now if he really had seen his mother, Mark thought, she would be accused of murder. For Andrew would not keep quiet. Why should he?

He felt her hands clutching at his jacket.

"You must finish him off, Mark," she mouthed. "Don't you see, if the Laird finds out—"

He put up his own hands and pulled hers away. He knew now for certain. She was mentally deranged. She had had only one thought when she had gone on to the cliff to push Andrew to his death.

She believed he, her son, should be heir

to Arachnock. It had been her poor, pathetic way of making sure that he was not cheated out of the inheritance she believed was his by right.

"You will do as I say, won't you, Mark?"

"Stay here, Mum!" he murmured. "Go and sit by the fire until I come back."

"But—you know what you must do?" she demanded.

He led her to a chair and sat her in it. He nodded and bent to kiss her.

"Yes, mother, I know what I must do!" he said and turned to the door.

18

DR. GORDON looked at the still figure on the bed; then he turned to Jean and Adam.

"He'll be all right now," he said. "It's a nasty fracture. It would have been impossible to set it without giving him a shot."

"How long will he stay unconscious?" Jean asked.

"Not very long. But he mustn't move." The doctor looked at Jean. "There ought to be someone with him tonight."

"I'll sit by him," she said.

"And I'll take over from you later," Adam said.

The two men went from the room.

"I wouldn't have thought a young man like that, with all his senses about him, would have taken a nose dive from the top of the cliff," the doctor said. "Lucky for him that ledge stopped his fall."

Adam said nothing to this. He was thinking of the talk he had had with Andrew as they waited to be rescued from the cliff by the coastguards.

If Mrs. Anderson really had tried to push Andrew to his death the Laird ought to be told.

"But perhaps Andrew had better tell him himself," he thought. "He's more likely to believe his grandson than me."

The doctor looked curiously at him as they went downstairs.

"That young lady we left with young Andrew," he said. "Didn't he arrive here with her yesterday?"

"Yes, they're—" Adam had been about to say "engaged," but stopped himself.

The doctor frowned.

"I think you know that Stuart Campbell died today?"

"Yes, I'm sorry. A heart attack, wasn't it?"

"I mention it because I've been with his daughter this evening. She told me that she and Andrew Murray were engaged to be married."

228

Adam looked at him in genuine astonishment. Matters had moved faster than he had realised.

"Are you sure, doctor?" he asked.

"I've known Fiona Campbell since she was a baby," Dr. Gordon said rather stiffly. "She isn't a liar. She's hardly likely to make up such a tale if it wasn't true."

Adam shook his head.

"I don't think Miss Clayton knows," he said.

"I gather the two young people decided to marry this afternoon," the other said. "I don't suppose young Murray's had a chance to speak to Miss Clayton since then."

Adam nodded. He supposed Andrew would tell Jean when he recovered consciousness. He wondered how she would react. Ought he to warn her what was coming?

He was not at all sure if this wasn't all for the best. Yet he had no reason to believe that Jean no longer loved Andrew —or, at least, that she was reconciled to

229

the fact that he did not love her. Whatever changes might have taken place in their feelings, so far as outsiders were concerned the only point at issue between them was whether or not they would get married, thus defying the Laird's wishes, and return to England together.

He had long believed that, faced with a choice, Andrew would have preferred to accept his grandfather's offer even if it meant breaking his engagement to Jean. If he had fallen in love with Fiona as well, that clinched the matter.

Not for the first time that day, Adam cursed the peculiar circumstances in which they were placed. It was so difficult for him to declare his own feelings for Jean, and he could not be certain they would be reciprocated.

"I'll just call and tell the Laird that I've set the broken arm," Dr. Gordon said in the hall.

He crossed to the study door, tapped on it, and when the Laird's gruff tones answered, went into the room.

Presently he came out and nodded at

Adam as the young man helped him into his overcoat.

"The poor chap's very shaken," he said. "I told him his grandson is in no danger and will be all the better for a good sleep."

"You didn't say anything about—Fiona Campbell and Andrew?" Adam asked.

The other shook his head.

"No, I thought it best to leave that for another to tell," he said with a chuckle. "Well, goodnight, my boy. If there are any complications give me a ring and I'll come right away. But Andrew's a healthy young man. I expect to find him a great deal better when I call tomorrow."

When he had gone Andrew hesitated. Ought he to talk to the Laird?

He was surprised that the old man had not come to Andrew's room when he had been told of the accident. The Laird was the sort of man who would want to know immediately what was going on, not sit moping in his study waiting for someone to bring scraps of information to him.

He made up his mind. Tapping on the

study door he opened it and looked into the big room.

The Laird was sitting at his desk in a pool of light from a lamp on his desk. The rest of the room was in shadow.

He looked up as Adam made for his desk. He did not speak and Adam, looking down at him, was shocked at the drawn features.

The Laird of Arachnock seemed to have aged ten years in the course of the last few hours.

Surely, Adam thought, the fact that his grandson had broken his arm could not have affected him so drastically.

"You'll have heard from the doctor about Andrew's accident, sir?" he said. "Evidently he'll be all right now the arm's been set."

The Laird nodded. His eyes were dull and full of misery.

"Yes, I heard," he muttered.

Thinking to cheer him up Adam said:

"Evidently Andrew asked Fiona Campbell to marry him today. You'd heard her father died this morning after a sudden heart attack."

Again the Laird nodded. Adam wondered at the old man's lack of response to this news, which capped his plans with success.

Everything was working out to his advantage. Fiona and Andrew were to marry, and therefore the Campbell acres would be added to the Laird's. All of Bleiside would shortly belong to the Murrays.

Yet something had happened, something that had struck at the old man's spirit. He was only a ghost of his old self.

"Is anything the matter, sir?" Adam asked anxiously.

Slowly the Laird raised lack-lustre eyes to his.

"Mark came to see me," he muttered.

Startled, Adam gasped:

"Mark! But—but I thought—"

"You thought he was still in prison—as I did," the Laird said, his voice the voice of a very old man. "But he was discharged a little earlier than expected

—some miscalculation on the part of the authorities, it would appear."

He gave a short harsh laugh.

"Ah, well, I suppose the prison authorities know what they are doing."

"When did he arrive on Bleiside?" Adam asked.

He thought suddenly of Fiona Campbell. She and Mark had been engaged. Perhaps he had seen her first and she had sent him away, then had got engaged to Andrew on the rebound.

"He came over to the island on the morning steamer," the Laird said. "He came to the castle—to see his mother."

"But—"

"Why did he come to see me?" the old man muttered. "He had no intention of doing so in the first place. So he told me and I don't doubt it's true. He had no other thought than to get some money out of his mother to set himself up in London. But something happened, something that sent him here to this study to see me."

234

Adam suddenly had an idea what that might be. But he did not speak.

"He came to see me to tell me that his mother tried to murder Andrew," the Laird said in a voice little more than a whisper. "He told me—she wanted Andrew out of the way so that I'd reinstate Mark as my heir. She came back to the castle believing Andrew was dead. It was only when she heard he was still alive, that he had been brought back to the castle, that she urged her son to finish off what she had started!"

The old man put trembling hands over his face. Adam took a step forward as if to comfort him. But there was little he could do or say. He waited.

The Laird lowered his hands and regarded Adam with grieving eyes.

"I told him that his mother had been in a mental home," the old man said. "He realised then that she cannot have been normal for some time, that this was not something that had come on her suddenly." He broke off, then added, "I should have paid more attention to her myself. To give Mark his due, he was full of remorse. He feels guilty because it was his behaviour that unbalanced his mother's reason in the first place."

The old man got slowly to his feet. He crossed to the window, pulled aside the curtain and looked out.

"He is going to take his mother away," he said. "He will take her back to the nursing home where they know all about her case. She will be happier there than here with Andrew occupying the place that she thinks her son should have had."

"Won't the police have something to say about it?"

The Laird shrugged. "If Andrew agrees they need not know."

"After that—what will Mark do?"

"I shall give him five thousand pounds to set himself up in business. He says he has ideas. But he will have to promise not to come back to Bleiside. I shall want you to draw up an agreement to that effect for him to sign."

After another short silence the Laird said:

"He told me he wanted to start a new life. He had no wish to be Laird of Arachnock." There was distaste in the old man's voice when he added: "He said, 'it wasn't his thing!' whatever that might mean."

"I shall go back to London tomorrow, sir," Adam said.

"You have the draft of my new will. And you will know how to word the agreement Mark must sign?"

Adam nodded. He said:

"I hope Andrew and Fiona will be happy. The only one I'm sorry for is Jean, the girl Andrew asked to marry him, the girl he thought you would accept as his wife."

The Laird shrugged.

"In life there is always someone who must suffer. I too am sorry for her. But she is the one who must make the sacrifice."

He looked up at Adam with a return of something like his old spirit.

"Perhaps it will not be such a sacrifice," he said, regarding Adam intently.

237

"Perhaps she has reason to feel glad she will not marry my grandson?"

Adam did not return the look. A moment later, he left the room. He went upstairs and paused outside Andrew's room.

Should he go in and talk to Jean as she kept her lonely vigil by the bedside?

But what would he tell her if he did? Was this the time or place to declare his own love for her—while they sat at the bedside of the man whom, until a matter of hours ago, she had been planning to marry?

With a sigh he turned away and went along to his own room. He would rest for a while then go along, as arranged, to relieve Jean.

19

JEAN must have nodded off. She wakened with a start and looked at the face, pale and drawn, against the pillow.

Andrew's eyes were open. They were looking at her. There was a puzzled frown on his forehead.

"Jean, what are you doing here! What's happened?" he muttered and put up his hand to his forehead.

"Lie still, Andrew," she said quietly. "You fell off the cliff. You have a broken arm. The doctor gave you a shot while he set the bone."

"I remember now." He put his sound arm under the covers again. "But why are you sitting with me? I'm not very bad, am I?"

She shook her head.

"The doctor said you mustn't be left tonight." She frowned. "I'm afraid I was dozing when you woke."

"I feel much better," he said. Then his face darkened. "It's coming back to me now. That woman pushed me off the cliff top."

"What woman?" she asked, puzzled.

"My aunt! She came up behind me when I was standing on top of the cliff. She gave me a shove and over I went."

"But—"

"Oh, it's hard to believe, I know," he said angrily. "But it's true, for all that. The woman's a murderess."

"But why would she do it?"

"Because I've supplanted her son in the Laird's eyes, and because she's mad, I suppose."

She did not know whether to believe him or not. Perhaps the fall had given him delusions. Maybe he had imagined that Mrs. Anderson had come up behind him and pushed him off the cliff.

The doctor, in passing, had said he could have struck his head though there had been no sign of a fracture—even a bruise—when he had examined his patient.

"Don't worry about it now, Andrew," she begged. "Try to sleep again. You'll feel better in the morning."

"But my grandfather should be told," he said excitedly. "There's a would-be murderess at large in the castle!"

"There, there," she said soothingly. "At least, leave it for the present. Everyone will be asleep by this time."

He caught her hand. His eyes were anxious now.

"There's something else, Jean," he said quietly.

"What is it?" she asked gently.

"It's about—us."

She nodded in a resigned way. At last he was going to tell her what she—and others—had guessed long ago. She wondered if he had gone out on to the cliffs in order to steel himself for what he was going to say to her—that he meant to make his home in Arachnock Castle, marry Fiona Campbell, and say goodbye to her for ever.

"Jean—I want you to release me from our engagement."

241

"You mean," she answered with a trace of a sly smile, "because your grandfather doesn't want you to marry me?"

He shook his head impatiently.

"No, Jean, it's nothing like that! It's nothing to do with my grandfather. You see, I—I've fallen in love with someone else."

She looked at him. There was a light in his grey eyes that she had never noticed before. He had fallen in love, at first sight almost, with Fiona Campbell. It was very different from the slow, easy way in which he had come to believe he loved her.

"It's Fiona Campbell," he said and looked away as if ashamed of meeting her eyes. "It happened this morning. I heard her father had had a heart attack and I went to her. I found that Mr. Campbell was dead."

"And in comforting Fiona you realised that you loved her, not me?"

She felt no bitterness, little sorrow even. Her main feeling, she realised with surprise, was one of relief. Her love for

242

Andrew, she could now recognise, had been fading since they had come to Bleiside Island, perhaps since he had first announced his intention of going—against his mother's wishes.

"Aren't you angry with me?" he asked.

She shook her head. She even managed to smile.

"No, I'm not angry," she said. "In a way, it's all worked out for the best. You've got a girl you really love and your grandfather will be happy because all along he must have wanted you to marry Fiona."

"But—you?"

Unexpectedly, she felt the prick of tears behind her eyes. She blinked them angrily away. But the tears were not because she had lost Andrew to another girl. It was the humiliation she felt at being unwanted by a man who had once told her he worshipped the very ground she trod on.

"I'm sorry," he muttered.

She put her hand over his and squeezed it.

"Go to sleep," she said. "I shall go

home tomorrow on the morning steamer. I'll often think of you here on Bleiside, lord of all you survey! I hope you'll be very happy."

He closed his eyes. Her tears made him feel guilty. He had thought he loved Jean. Until he met Fiona. The thought of Fiona's sweet face filled his mind. He fell asleep again, a smile on his lips.

When Adam relieved Jean he asked her if Andrew had wakened.

"Just for a few moments," she replied. "He soon went to sleep again."

"You'd better go and get some rest," he murmured. "You look tired out."

She gave him a grateful smile and made for the door. When she had gone he sat by the bed and looked down at the sleeping man.

Had he imagined it or had there been tears in Jean's eyes? He wondered what had passed between her and Andrew when he had wakened. Had he told her about his aunt who had so nearly succeeded in killing him?

Then he sighed and settled down to his

vigil. What would tomorrow bring? Was he doomed to return to his lonely life in London, a life which would never be the same again thanks to the last two days on Bleiside Island? Something in Jean's face as she had said good-night, told him it might not be quite like that.

In the morning the doctor came early to the castle.

After he had examined Andrew he told the Laird that his patient could get up later in the day. All traces of shock and exhaustion had been thrown off by the healthy young man. His broken arm would do nicely in a sling.

The steamer sailed at eleven o'clock. Adam spent some time with the Laird in his study. The old man told him that Mark and his mother would be travelling the following day.

"There are several arrangements to be made," Mr. Murray said. "Mark tells me he has persuaded his mother to go back to the nursing home. I'm better pleased with the young man than I thought I would be, though I'll never, never forgive him for dragging the Murray name through the mud of the criminal courts."

"I'll see he has the money you've promised him," Adam said. "He'll come round to my office in due course and I'll find out exactly what he has in mind."

The old man held out his hand.

"You're a good friend to the Murrays, Adam Simmonds, as your father was before ye. And now be on your way. The Rolls is waiting to take you to Bleiside to catch the steamer."

Adam went out into the big hall. He had earlier said goodbye to Andrew. He had not seen Jean who had had breakfast in her room. Suddenly, the thought struck him with something like panic that she might not be leaving on the same steamer.

Mrs. Baird came into the hall.

"Have you seen Miss Clayton?" he asked.

She shook her head though there was a twinkle in her eyes.

"She must be somewhere about," she

246

said and hid a chuckle as he turned away.

"I'll have to go or I'll miss the steamer," he said.

They shook hands and he hurried out of the hall, down the steps to the courtyard where Douggie MacLean with the Rolls was waiting.

The chauffeur opened the door and Adam stepped into the big car's dark interior.

Suddenly he realised that someone else was sitting on the back seat. His heart leapt.

"Jean!" he exclaimed. "I thought—"

"You thought I was staying for tomorrow's steamer, I suppose," she said. "There was no point. I suppose you know that Andrew will be marrying Fiona Campbell?"

"Yes, I did know."

As the big car left the courtyard and went down the slope outside to the road he said:

"I'm sorry things had to end like this."

She shook her head.

"Don't be sorry for me, Adam," she

said and as the car increased its pace she looked round at the desolate landscape, moor on one side, sea and sand on the other. "I would never have settled here. I'm sure of that now."

"And Andrew—?"

She smiled. "Andrew came into my life when I was very lonely. I know now that I never really loved him."

She turned to face him, and her delicate face, framed in soft honey-brown waves, filled him with powerful feelings in which it was hard to separate his desire for her from his wish to protect her from ever being hurt again.

"You know," he began hesitantly, "I'm just a boring lawyer—"

"Oh Adam!" Her full red lips curled into a smile. "Lawyer you may be. Boring never!"

She smiled up into his earnest face, into those bright blue eyes with their message of love and sympathy. Gently, he took her hand in his. She remembered how frightened she had been to see him lowering himself courageously down the cliff the night before to make sure Andrew was safe.

She had hardly thought of Andrew then, cold, frightened and hurt though he was. It had been Adam's safety that concerned her.

Impulsively she squeezed Adam's hand. He put his other arm around her shoulders and, very softly, kissed her on the lips.

Douggie MacLean, eye on the rear-view mirror, narrowly avoided crumpling the wing of the Rolls on the stone wall lining the road.

They sat quietly together at the back of the big Rolls, quietly happy in each other's company, the future shining as brightly as the morning sunlight on the calm waters of the sound.

THE EIGHTH NURSE
by Jill Murray

What makes a girl become a nurse? Matron and Sister Tutor often discussed it and this last batch of eight were a terrible lot. The girls themselves had all joined for a variety of reasons, and mostly for the wrong ones. They were, for the most part, a lively lot, but the eighth nurse was different.

TUG OF WAR
by Sue Peters

There was absolutely no reason why Dee Lawrence's and Nat Archer's paths should cross—but somehow they did, to Dee's dismay and fury. For every time they met the sparks flew—and what was far worse, Nat always managed to get the better of her.

LOVE BE WARY
by Mary Raymond

The holiday of a lifetime with no complications—that was what Beth Graham had imagined her stay on the Italian Riviera would be. But of course she hadn't bargained for Ben Eliot and Eddie Ricquier, nor for the stormy emotions the two men would arouse in her.

THE SIN OF CYNARA
by Violet Winspear

Five-year-old Teri was not Carol's child but her sister Cynara's—although Carol's husband Vincenzo had been his father—but she had always looked upon him as her own child. She was determined to do her best for him, even if she had to beg the help of Vincenzo's family.

WITH SOMEBODY ELSE
by Theresa Charles

Rosamond sets off for Cornwall with Hugo to meet his family, blissfully unaware of the shocks in store for her.

A SUMMER FOR STRANGERS
by Claire Hamilton

Because she had lost her job, her flat and she had no money, Tabitha agreed to pose as Adam's future wife although she believed the scheme to be deceitful and cruel.

VILLA OF SINGING WATER
by Angela Petron

The disquieting incidents that occurred at the Vatican and the Colosseum did not unnecessarily trouble Jan at first, but then they became increasingly unpleasant and alarming.

DOCTOR NAPIER'S NURSE
by Pauline Ash
When cousins Midge and Derry are entered as probationer nurses on the same day but at different hospitals they agree to exchange identities.

A GIRL LIKE JULIE
by Louise Ellis
Caroline absolutely adored Hugh Barrington, but then Julie Crane came into their lives. Julie was the kind of girl who attracts men without even trying.

COUNTRY DOCTOR
by Paula Lindsay
When Evan Richmond bought a practice in a remote country village he did not realise that a casual encounter would lead to the loss of his heart.

ENCORE
by Helga Moray

Craig and Janet realise that their true happiness lies with each other, but it is only under traumatic circumstances that they can be reunited.

NICOLETTE
by Ivy Preston

When Grant Alston came back into her life, Nicolette was faced with a dilemma. Should she follow the path of duty or the path of love?

THE GOLDEN PUMA
by Margaret Way

Catherine's time was spent looking after her father's Queensland farm. But what life was there without David, who wasn't interested in her?

HOSPITAL BY THE LAKE
by Anne Durham

Nurse Marguerite Ingleby was always ready to become personally involved with her patients, to the despair of Brian Field, the Senior Surgical Registrar, who loved her.

VALLEY OF CONFLICT
by David Farrell

Isolated in a hostel in the French Alps, Ann Russell sees her fiancé being seduced by a young girl. Then comes the avalanche that imperils their lives.

NURSE'S CHOICE
by Peggy Gaddis

A proposal of marriage from the incredibly handsome and wealthy Reagan was enough to upset any girl—and Brooke Martin was no exception.

A DANGEROUS MAN
by Anne Goring
Photographer Polly Burton was on safari in Monbasa when she met enigmatic Leon Hammond. But unpredictability was the name of the game where Leon was concerned.

PRECIOUS INHERITANCE
by Joan Moules
Karen's new life working for an authoress took her from Sussex to a foreign airstrip and a kidnapping; to a real life adventure as gripping as any in the books she typed.

VISION OF LOVE
by Grace Richmond
When Kathy takes over the run-down country kennels she finds Alec Stinton, a local vet, very helpful. But their friendship arouses bitter jealousy and a tragedy seems inevitable.

CRUSADING NURSE
by Jane Converse

It was handsome Dr. Corbett who opened Nurse Susan Leighton's eyes and who set her off on a lonely crusade against some powerful enemies and a shattering struggle against the man she loved.

WILD ENCHANTMENT
by Christina Green

Rowan's agreeable new boss had a dream of creating a famous perfume using her precious Silverstar, but Rowan's plans were very different.

DESERT ROMANCE
by Irene Ord

Sally agrees to take her sister Pam's place as La Chartreuse the dancer, but she finds out there is more to it than dyeing her hair red and looking like her sister.

HEART OF ICE
by Marie Sidney

How was January to know that not only would the warmth of the Swiss people thaw out her frozen heart, but that she too would play her part in helping someone to live again?

LUCKY IN LOVE
by Margaret Wood

Melanie, companion-secretary to the wealthy Laura Duxford, had lost her heart to Laura's son, Julian. Someone was trying to get Laura—a compulsive gambler—thrown out of the Casino, someone who would even resort to murder.

NURSE TO PRINCESS JASMINE
by Lilian Woodward

Nick's surgeon brother, Tom, performs an operation on an Arabian princess, and she invites Tom, Nick and his fiancé to Omander, where a web of deceit and intrigue closes about the three young people.

THE WAYWARD HEART
by Eileen Barry

Disaster-prone Katherine's nickname was "Kate Calamity". She was a good natured girl, but her boss went too far with an outrageous proposal, because of her latest disaster, she could not refuse.

FOUR WEEKS IN WINTER
by Jane Donnelly

Tessa wasn't looking forward to going back to her old home town and meeting Paul Mellor again—she had made a fool of herself over him once before. But was Orme Jared's solution to her problem likely to be the right one?

SURGERY BY THE SEA
by Sheila Douglas

Medical student Meg hadn't really wanted to leave London and her boy-friend to go and work with a G.P. on the Welsh coast for the summer, although the job had its compensations. But Owen Roberts was certainly not one of them!

HEAVEN IS HIGH
by Anne Hampson

The new heir to the Manor of Marbeck had been found—an American from the Rocky Mountains! But it was rather unfortunate that when he arrived unexpectedly he found an uninvited guest, complete with Stetson and high boots, singing "I'm an old cowhand . . . Here I am, straight from those jolly ole Rockies . . ."

LOVE WILL COME
by Sarah Devon

June Baker's boss was not really her idea of her ideal man, but when she went from third typist to boss's secretary overnight she began to change her mind.

ESCAPE TO ROMANCE
by Kay Winchester

Oliver and Jean first met on Swale Island. They were both trying to begin their lives afresh, but neither had bargained for complications from the past.

CASTLE IN THE SUN
by Cora Mayne

Emma's invalid sister, Kym, needed a warm climate, and Emma jumped at the chance of a job on a Mediterranean island looking after another girl of Kym's age. But it wasn't that easy. Emma soon finds that intrigues and hazards lurk on the sunlit isle.

BEWARE OF LOVE
by Kay Winchester

Carol Brampton resumes her nursing career when her husband and daughter are killed in a car accident. With the help of Dr. Patrick Farrell she begins to pick up the pieces of her life, but is bitterly hurt when insinuations are made about her to Patrick.

DESERT DOCTOR
by Violet Winspear

Madeline felt that Morocco was a place made for love and romance, but unfortunately Doctor Victor Tourelle seemed to be unaffected by its romantic spell.

THE PRICE OF PARADISE
by Jane Arbor

It was a shock to Fern to meet her estranged husband Grant Wilder again, on an island in the middle of the Indian Ocean, but to discover that her father had engineered it puzzled Fern. What did he hope to achieve?

DOCTOR IN PLASTER
by Lisa Cooper

When Dr. Scott Sutcliffe is injured in a car accident, Nurse Caroline Hurst has to cope with a very demanding private case. But when she realises her exasperating patient has stolen her heart, how can Caroline possibly stay?

SAFARI ENCOUNTER
by Rosemary Carter

Jenny had to accept that she couldn't run her father's game park alone; that she would have to let forceful Joshua Adams virtually take over. But Jenny's real problem began when Joshua took over her heart as well!

ROMANTIC LEGACY
by Cora Mayne

As kennelmaid to the Armstrongs, Ann Brown, had no idea that she would become the central figure in a web of mystery and intrigue. Learning the truth about her father had an unforseen effect on her future, but in spite of everything she at last finds happiness.

THE RELENTLESS TIDE
by Jill Murray

Steve Palmer shared Nurse Marie Blane's love of the sea and small boats. Marie's other passion was her stepbrother. But when danger threatened who should she turn to—her stepbrother or the man who stirred emotions in her heart?

ROMANCE IN NORWAY
by Cora Mayne

Nancy Crawford hopes that her visit to Norway will help her to start life again. She certainly finds many surprises there, including unexpected happiness.